PENNY'S SECRET LOVE

AN AMISH ROMANCE

Naomi Troyer

Contents

Chapter 1
Extinguishing Hope

Penny Hershberger had never felt happier.

It felt as if she was walking on air, her heart bursting with joy and excitement for the future that lay ahead.

When Seth Mast, her sweetheart, had taken her on a buggy ride this afternoon, she had expected nothing but to spend time with him. The last thing she had expected was that Seth would go down on one knee and ask for her hand in marriage.

At seventeen, Penny felt as if her whole life lay ahead of her with a perfect future just waiting for her. Tomorrow she would be baptized in church as an official member of the community. Tomorrow she would take her vows to obey the ordnung, and tomorrow evening she would attend her first ever singing, with Seth, of course.

Seth could've waited till after her baptism to propose, but his excuse was that he wanted her to be his before anyone at Sunday singing got it into their mind to steal her away.

It was just like Seth to be charming and protective of her at the same time. That was why she had fallen in love with him in the spring. They had known each other all their lives, but over the last few months, Seth had stolen her heart with wildflowers and picnics. He had painted a future for them that Penny couldn't wait to embrace.

All she had to do now was to tell her parents of the good news. The last thing she needed was for the bishop to announce their engagement in church tomorrow and for her parents to be surprised.

She all but bounced into the kitchen, eager to share the wonderful news with her parents. Penny might be young, but she wasn't naïve. She knew that some waited all their lives to experience the joy of love. She was blessed to have found it early in her life.

"Mamm, where's Daed?" Penny asked as soon as she spotted her mother in the kitchen.

"He's in the living room. Why?" Sarah Hershberger asked with a curious frown at the sight of her daughter's smile.

"I have news, Mamm, gut news," Penny revealed with a beaming smile. "Let me just ask Daed to join us."

Her mother laughed wholeheartedly. "If you're so happy, it must be gut news."

"It is!" Penny assured her before she went to fetch her father.

Once they were all seated around the kitchen table, Penny drew in a deep breath. The kitchen table was where everything happened in their house. It was where bible study was held, where problems were discussed, and where every meal was enjoyed. Penny knew that some called the kitchen the heart of the home, but for Penny, the kitchen table was the very beat of their family.

"So tell us?" her mother urged excitedly.

Penny smiled at her mother before she turned to her father. "Tomorrow in church the bishop is going to make an announcement after my baptism…" Penny trailed off for dramatic effect. "He is going to announce that Seth and I are engaged."

Her mother's smile brightened even as she clapped her hands together with glee. "Penny! That's wunderbaar!"

Her father's hand fell onto the table with a loud thump. Silence fell over the kitchen table as Penny and her mother turned to her father with confused expressions.

"When your mamm told me you were courting, I thought nothing of it. You're only still just a child. I let it be, since it seemed to make you happy. But I will not sit here and express my joy at an engagement."

"Daed?" Penny asked, confused. "What do you mean, you let it be?"

"I mean you are only seventeen years old. You haven't even been baptized and already you want to take another vow. You're too young, Penny, and as for Seth, don't even let me get started on the Mast fellow." Her father's voice was filled with condemnation and disappointment.

"Susannah, Clara, and Mamm were married before they turned eighteen. Why is it wrong for me to want to do the same?" Penny asked, hating the way her father looked at her.

"Because I could provide for your mamm. What can Seth Mast provide for you? Nothing. Barely a bed in his parents' house. No dochder of mine will get married without gut prospects for the future. I will not give my blessing for this engagement."

"Abram, please be reasonable. If this is what Penny wants…"

"Hold your tongue, frau," her father cried out abruptly. "I am the head of this haus. Either you accept my decision or you'll face the wrath of the ordnung," Abram warned his wife.

Penny's eyes nearly popped out of her head. She has never heard her father threaten her mother in that way. Instead of arguing, she tried pleading instead. "Daed, please. He makes me happy. He's going to become a carpenter one day, Daed. I'd like to support his dreams."

"You don't even know what love or dreams are. You're too young to even understand what a marriage will entail. Nee! That's my final decision. The engagement is to be broken off before your baptismal vows in the morning. Is that clear?"

Penny's breath caught even as she felt her heart shattered into a million different pieces. "You want me to break off the engagement?"

Her father nodded firmly. "You heard me."

"What if… what if I don't want to?" Penny asked quietly.

"Then you'll be disobeying your daed. You'll be breaking the ten commandments. Is that really how you want to start your life in this community?" Abram demanded in a loud voice.

Tears streamed over Penny's face as she shook her head. "Nee, Daed. Please… please don't do this."

"It's done. Now clean up this mess you've made. You should've known better than to accept. Seth Mast can't offer you anything and that is no way to begin a marriage. When you meet a man that can care for you, a man with more to his name than just a dream, I might be more open to giving my blessing."

Her father stood up and walked out of the kitchen, leaving Penny in tears and her mother stunned by his outburst.

For the first time in her life, Penny didn't want to obey her father. For the first time, she realized her father wasn't always right.

In fact, he couldn't have been more wrong if he tried.

Chapter 2
A Thorn in Her Side

7 years later

"My mamm insists I do this myself, but I'm a horrible seamstress," Mary Yoder gushed as Penny kneeled in front of her with a bowl of pins.

"I'm glad I can help," Penny said as she tucked in the seam to shorten it. Most Amish women sewed their own clothes, but there were women who preferred to go to a local seamstress and have them do the tedious chore of making clothes instead.

Mary Yoder was one of the latter.

"If it wasn't for you, I'd have pin pricks all over my fingers and blood all over the fabric." Mary laughed at her own joke. "Luckily, I have many other talents that redeem me."

Penny smiled, but didn't voice her thoughts. One of Mary's best talents was to gossip. As the daughter of one of the wealthiest farmers in the community, Mary had a lot of time on her hands. With most of the chores at home taken care of by her mother and older sister, Mary used her time to keep up with the latest happenings in the community.

Mary's gossip had offended many people in the community in the past, but luckily her gossip had never included Penny.

Penny lived a quiet life, still at home with her parents. Between the chores and sewing, she barely had any time to do anything newsworthy.

Becoming a seamstress had never been her dream, but after Seth left, Penny had turned to sewing to occupy her rambling thoughts and to ease her broken heart. When one of her friends had asked her to sew a new dress for her wedding, she had flattered Penny. Soon after, more orders rolled in, one after the other.

Before Penny even realized it, she had become a seamstress with an income that contributed to the household. She had never thought of seeking other employment since she enjoyed working from home and spending her days surrounded by fabric, thread, and silence.

When she wasn't sewing, she offered services as a cleaning lady, only for members of the community. Some of the older folks couldn't manage on their own and asked Penny to come in once a month just to give their homes a good clean.

Just like with the sewing, it was a way for Penny to earn an income without having to talk all the time. She could focus on cleaning and be rewarded with the results afterwards.

There were days that the silence became a little overwhelming. Days when she found herself lost in the past and the memories of Seth. Ever since he had left to become a carpenter's apprentice, he had never returned to the community again. Penny often wondered if he had found love and gotten married since he had left.

Did he have children?

Did he still think of her?

But thoughts like that didn't contribute to anything but more sadness.

After her parents had forced her to break off her engagement with Seth, Mary had all but given up on love. She didn't see the point in attending Sunday singings, only to confirm what she already knew.

No one would ever make her feel the way Seth had made her feel.

When she had turned twenty-one, her father had encouraged her to attend singings, but Penny refused. She had overheard her mother confess to her father once that she was becoming a hermit and a spinster, but not even that bothered Penny.

Few people would understand that her life had stopped having meaning the morning before her baptism. She could still remember the shock in Seth's eyes, his pleading tone to go against her father's wishes. He had begged her to leave with him for Indiana and to start a new life there, but Penny had abided by her parents' wishes and had wished him farewell before she had turned her back on him.

Just remembering that morning made Penny relive the heartache.

"There, that length is perfect," Mary said approvingly from above her.

"Gut," Penny nodded as she continued to pin the hem of the dress.

"Have you heard about Ruth Ebersohn? She's with boppli. Of course, they haven't made it public just yet. She's only two months along and after losing her first, they're keeping it quiet," Mary said in hushed tones.

Penny sighed inwardly. Ruth's news was hers to share and not Mary's to distribute. "If they're keeping it quiet, how do you know?"

"I saw her buying prenatal vitamins at the drugstore. Of course, I expressed my interest, and she told me all about the arrival of a bundle of joy," Mary admitted with a gleeful smile. "I don't know why, but people just love to confide in me."

Penny frowned, knowing that Mary couldn't see her face. The only reason anyone confided in her was because Mary's probing questions were about as subtle as a horse in a porcelain factory.

"You should really come to singings, Penny. You know, all the men are talking about you as an old maid," Mary warned.

Penny looked up at Mary with a curious look. "Is that supposed to bother me?"

"Not if you don't want a mann or a familye?" Mary asked with a cocked brow. "I might not be married yet, but at least I'm putting myself out there at every Sunday singing."

Penny smiled brightly and quickly changed the subject. The last person she was going to reveal her broken dreams with was Mary Yoder. "There you go, you can change. I'll have it done for you by tomorrow."

"Could you bring it in at the waist as well? I've just lost so much weight; it's hanging on me like an empty flour bag," Mary said, tucking in the sides of the dress at her waist.

It wasn't custom for plain dresses to be tight-fitting, but Penny wasn't about to give Mary a lecture on acceptable styles. "Of course."

Penny stood up and carefully pinned down one side of the dress before she moved to the other side. Just as she pinned the other side, Mary set off on another ramble of gossip again.

"You will never guess who returned to town. Go on, just guess?" Mary encouraged her.

Penny shook her head. "Tell me."

"Seth Mast," Mary announced. "Ouch! You stabbed me!"

Penny quickly withdrew the needle and took a step back. Penny felt the blood drain from her face as her heart raced. Hopefully Mary would see her reaction as one of apology for stabbing her with a needle. "I'm so sorry. How clumsy of me."

"It's fine, just be more careful," Mary said firmly before she continued to chatter. "His father passed away two days ago; did you hear?"

Penny frowned. "Nee, I hadn't."

For the first time, Penny wished she came out a little more.

"Jah, in his sleep. They found him yesterday morning. Horrible really. So Seth is back and here to deal with his father's affairs," Mary explained.

Penny felt her head spin and wished Mary could just stop talking. All this talk about Seth being back confused Penny more than she expected. It brought all those feelings racing back, all the heartache and the anger at her father for forcing her to break off the engagement.

"There, all done, you can go change now," Penny said again.

Mary nodded. "Denke. Tomorrow you say?"

"Jah," Penny agreed. She watched as Mary walked down the hallway to change and sat down in the closest chair.

She shook her head, struggling to fathom what Mary had just said. It had been seven years since she had last seen Seth Mast.

Now he was back.

Chapter 3
Return to
Broken Dreams

Seth had arrived in Lancaster County the day before. The bus journey from Indiana had been long and tiring, but what had been more exhausting had been the memories of Lancaster County that had returned to him ever since boarding the bus.

He had gone straight to his father's home from the bus stop, too tired to even consider going to see the bishop first. He had passed a few familiar faces on the way home, but didn't stop to accept their condolences on the passing of his father.

When Seth had received the news of his father's passing, the news hadn't only been shocking, but had brought with it so many regrets.

When he had left Lancaster County seven years ago, it had always been his intention to return. It had taken him three years of cancelling visits to his father, before he realized that too many memories were in Lancaster County. He simply couldn't face coming back here ever again.

Instead, he had bought his father a bus ticket to come and visit him twice a year in Indiana. Now he couldn't help but regret that he hadn't seen his father more often.

Except for his father and his childhood, Lancaster County only held heartbreak for him. When he thought of the town he had grown up in, the fields he had played in, and the creeks where he had swum on hot summer days, every memory was interspersed with a memory of Penny.

Seth knew they had been young, but to this day, he knew that the love he had felt for Penny would've lasted them a lifetime. Even without seeing her for seven years, simply the thought of her still made his heart ache with regret.

For the last seven years, he had spent all his energy and time on perfecting his skills as a carpenter. He had opened his own workshop and had made a good name for himself. The young man with nothing to his name but a dream was long gone; instead Seth was living his dream of becoming a carpenter and making a good living from it.

The only problem was he had no one to share it with.

After finishing his cup of coffee, he headed out to the barn to hitch the horse to the buggy. He couldn't delay seeing the bishop any longer. The sooner his father was buried and his affairs dealt with, the sooner Seth could return to the life he had built for himself.

The life without Penny.

A life that offered no reminders of the girl that had stolen his heart.

A few times over the years, Seth had met a woman that had caught his eye. Every time he had hoped that perhaps she would be the woman to heal his heart from losing

Penny. That she would be the woman he could build a life with, have children with, and share his achievements with.

But no woman had ever held up to the high standards Penny had set for his heart. No woman had ever made his heart swell with joy or skip in anticipation of seeing her smile.

For that reason, Seth had never asked a woman on a second buggy ride.

About a year ago, he had given up on buggy rides altogether.

He drove the horse towards the bishop's home, wishing there was another route he could've taken. A route that wouldn't take him past the Hershberger homestead. As the homestead came into view, Seth felt his heart grow heavy with remorse.

He had spent so much time there with Penny, so many happy memories that it pained him to even look in that direction.

He kept his eyes firmly on the road, reminding himself that seven years had passed. Penny's parents might not have approved of him, but by now they must have approved of a suitable husband for their daughter.

He didn't doubt for a single moment that Penny would be married with kinner of her own. She had probably forgotten all about the boy whose heart she had broken one fateful Sunday morning. The boy whose life she had changed irrevocably.

That day had not only left Seth heartbroken, but it had left him doubting love.

How could someone that claimed to love you simply turn you away?

A heavy sigh escaped him as he called to the horse to step up into a gallop. The sooner he dealt with his father's affairs, the sooner he could leave.

Hopefully before he saw Penny Hershberger, or the happy family she no doubt had.

Chapter 4
The Woman in the Shadows

News of Seth's return to the community spread just as quickly as word about his father's funeral. Just like with any other member of the community, it was an unspoken rule that everyone in the community would attend the funeral.

Penny had considered pretending to be ill the morning of the funeral. She couldn't stand the thought of seeing Seth again after what she had said to him the last time they had seen each other. She had known that he wouldn't accept her shallow excuses for breaking up their engagement and eventually had told him the truth.

She had told him that her father didn't approve of Seth because he wasn't wealthy enough to provide for her. Because his daughter deserved better.

Shame washed over Penny at the memory.

How could she face him knowing what hurtful things she had said?

But, curiosity had won.

For the last seven years, she had often thought of Seth and the life he had built for himself in Indiana, and now for the first time she could see him again. She was curious what he would look like and if he would still be the same boy she had fallen in love with all those years ago.

Although she wanted to see him, Penny didn't want him to see her. She was ashamed of how she had treated him and didn't want to be a reminder of that horrible time on the day Seth buried his father.

That's why she remained hidden during the funeral. When she wasn't bowing her head to remain out of sight, she stood behind someone tall.

Only when they stood around the grave of old Mr. Mast did Penny really catch her first glimpse of Seth. Her heart vaulted in her chest, skipping the shame and the regrets, right back to the feelings Seth had awakened in her all those years ago.

If it was possible, he had become even more handsome than he had been.

His jaw was masculine, his eyes hooded with thick brows. His shoulders were broad and even from where she stood, she could see his hands were calloused from hard work.

Did Seth become the carpenter he had set out to be?

Dozens of questions raced through her mind as watched him from the shadows. She wondered why his wife didn't come to support him during this time of need and wished she could've stood next to him to support him instead.

But being by Seth's side wasn't her place.

Instead, her place was here, hidden by other people, and watching him from afar.

For a long time Penny had thought she had gotten over Seth, but now she realized she hadn't. She glanced at her father only a short distance away and realized she hadn't forgiven her father, either.

Today was supposed to be a day of mourning for losing a life, but along with mourning the loss of Seth's father, Penny mourned the love she would never have.

Because in that moment, she realized she would never find the same love with anyone as she had had with Seth.

The realization was startling, to say the least.

Penny gasped softly.

"Are you alright?" her best friend, Anna Miller, asked her with a curious look.

Penny quickly nodded. "Jah, I'm fine."

Anna cocked her brow with a curious look. Her long-time friend, was the only person who knew how hard Penny had taken breaking off her engagement. Anna was the only person who understood how it jaded Penny's view of life and love.

Although Anna had married and had four beautiful children, Anna never shied away from their friendship. Anna was constantly encouraging Penny to open her heart to love again. Anna was the only person who knew that Penny hid behind sewing and cleaning to busy her mind and her body to stop herself from thinking about the life she had really wanted.

A life with Seth.

Anna reached for her hand and squeezed it tightly, understanding how hard it was for Penny to see Seth again. She didn't say a single word, instead, her quiet support was all that Penny needed.

When the service was finally over, the funeral goers headed to the bishop's house to commiserate with Seth and his loss, but Penny escaped, claiming she had a headache.

She could see her mother didn't completely believe her, but she also wasn't up to explaining to her mother why she couldn't go.

Instead, she walked all the way home in tears, dreaming of what could've been if only she hadn't obeyed her father.

Even now, Penny couldn't imagine going against her father's wishes. But she still wondered if her father had ever realized how much his decision had affected her life.

Did he regret it at all?

Chapter 5
Chaos & Children

"Ach Penny, thank heavens you came," Anna said, opening the door with an exhausted expression. The pallor of her skin leaned towards green, with dark purple shadows beneath her eyes.

"Of course," Penny said quickly as she stepped into the Miller home.

Anna usually kept a perfectly neat house. Regardless of having four children, all of whom were under the age of six, everything had its place and there was never a speck of dust to be seen.

Whereas now, chaos surrounded Penny, a clear sign that her friend needed help. A quick glance towards the kitchen revealed unwashed dishes piled high beside the sink. Splatters on the floor revealed it hadn't been washed in days. Toys were scattered all over the living room, with blankets tossed on the couches as if everyone had been sleeping there instead of in their beds.

"It's a nightmare!" Anna admitted as tears welled in her eyes. "It started right after the funeral, a bug of some sort. My stomach has been upset for three days now and nothing seems to help."

"You poor thing, that's terrible," Penny commiserated.

"Jah, it is. But what's even worse is that I need medicine and I can't go into town. The twins both have the flu, and I need medicine for them as well. And John…. John simply isn't managing." Anna sniffed. "I didn't know what else to do."

Penny smiled encouragingly. "You did the right thing. Why don't you get right back into bed and I'll make you some tea and toast? As soon as I've cleaned the kitchen, I'll go into town and get what you need."

"Denke Penny. But you don't have to go alone. John wants to go. He needs a few things as well, but he's afraid of taking all the kinner with him."

"Then the kinner can stay and I'll take care of them while you rest." Penny quickly solved all Anna's problems. But instead of being rewarded with a smile, Anna sniffed.

"The twins… they need to see the doctor and the other two… I just need to sleep, Penny," Anna all but pleaded.

Penny understood. She wasn't here just to clean and babysit, she had to accompany John into town so that Anna could rest while everyone was away. Penny rested her hands on her friend's shoulders. "Then I'll go with John and *all* the kinner. Now you get back into bed. That's an order."

"You're a gut friend, Penny." Anna smiled gratefully.

Penny hushed her before shooing her off to bed. She found John and the children doing chores in the yard. The twins were six years old, both had red noses and swollen eyes. No doubt a cold or a flu that was taking hold. The other two children, aged four and two, seemed healthy as horses as they chased the chickens around the yard.

"Penny, thank heavens you came. I wasn't sure you would." John expressed his gratitude the moment he spotted Penny.

"Of course I would. I'm going to clean the kitchen and set the living room back to rights. We can leave for town in about an hour. Will that work for you?" Penny asked.

John nodded. "Perfect."

Penny headed back to the house and began in the kitchen. It was a good thing she spent a lot of time visiting Anna, so she knew where everything came. A half an hour later, all the dishes were washed and put away, and the kitchen floor had been washed.

Next she moved into the living room, putting away blankets and toys as she went.

Exactly an hour later, she stepped outside to see John had already hitched the buggy. "I just need to fetch the kinder, then we can leave."

Penny nodded. "The twins are in the living room. I'll get them."

"Denke, I think Rebecca went to show Joseph the flowers in the field out back." John headed around the barn while Penny went to fetch the twins.

After a quick word with Anna about what medicine she should get for her, Penny met John and the other two children outside. "Are you ready?"

John nodded. "I ought to ask you that. Have you ever been to town with four children? Where you're not running after one, you're trying to stop another from running away. I swear my children forget all their manners as soon as we stop in town."

"They'll be just fine. Do you have an appointment at the Englisch doctor for the twins?"

"Nee, the clinic. The doctor isn't consulting today. The clinic said the nurse would look at them and tell me what they need."

"Very well then. I've also made a list of everything you need in the kitchen." Penny handed John the list as she climbed into the buggy. "There's also a few things on there I'll need to cook dinner."

"You don't have to cook us dinner," John argued.

Penny smiled and shook her head. "John, I've just done the dishes. You and your kinner can't' live on bread and eggs. I'll cook a stew before I leave; a gut meal might do Anna some gut as well."

"She's right you know. You are the best friend a woman could have."

Penny laughed. "She would do the same for me. Now let's get going so we can get back."

They had barely driven out of the yard when the twins began to bicker. "It's my ribbon."

"Nee, it's my ribbon."

"I saw it first."

"I took it first."

"Boys! Enough," Penny said firmly over her shoulder. "Either you take turns to play with the ribbon, or I'll cut it in half so you each have a piece."

Both Levi and Daniel's eyes widened at her stern tone. Although they had grown up right before her eyes, it was the first time Penny felt the need to scold them.

"Uh, alright Penny," Levi finally said before giving the ribbon to Daniel. "Here you go. You can play with it first."

John chuckled beside Penny. "That is a gift. You should nurture it for when you have children someday. They adore you."

Penny smiled but didn't comment. She had long since given up on having children.

She had given up on that the day she walked away from Seth.

Chapter 6
A Happy Familye

"Denke for meeting me." Seth stood up as the Englischer introduced himself.

"It's my pleasure. It's not very often I'm contacted by someone in your community. Usually property sales in the Amish community are conducted privately," Brandon Williams explained as he took a seat across from Seth in the coffee shop.

Seth shrugged. "I know, but I don't have time to find out who might be interested and then to negotiate a price, only to turn down a barter. I need to get back to Indiana."

"Are you the sole inheritor of your father's estate?" Brandon asked, opening a folder of notes and forms.

"That's right, jah. As I live in Indiana, it makes no sense for me to keep the property here," Seth explained.

It had been five days since his father's funeral and it felt as if everything was moving at a snail's pace. Something was hurrying Seth to return to Indiana and although he refused to admit it, that something was the fear of seeing Penny again.

For the last week, he had avoided seeing her. He didn't even see her at his father's funeral, which could only mean that if she knew he was back, she wasn't eager to see him either. Not that Seth was mad at her, but he feared that if he saw Penny Hershberger again, it would take him another seven years to try to forget her.

Something he hadn't even achieved during the first seven years.

"Do you own the property in Indiana?" Brandon asked curiously as he began jotting down notes on a piece of paper.

"Nee, I'm leasing a property there."

"So you intend to purchase that property with the proceeds from this sale?"

Seth frowned. "I'm not sure what I intend to do. I just know I need to deal with my father's estate so I can return home. Now how long will it take before you can put the property in the market?"

"I can do that as soon as I see the property. Of course, I'll need to take a few photos and take a few measurements, but from what you mentioned over the phone, I can't imagine the price will be less than what you were hoping for." Brandon paused when a waitress stopped by their table. "Tall skim latte with cinnamon."

"Of course and for you, sir?" the waitress asked, turning to Seth.

"Just kaffe please, black, no sugar," Seth replied with a smile before he turned back to Brandon. "I want to make sure Amish folk buys the property. The community would never forgive me if I sell to the Englisch."

Brandon let out a sigh. "I'll do my best. I'll put up the for-sale signs at all the local businesses the Amish communities frequent, then we can cross our fingers that it's snatched up soon."

"Denke."

"Right, now let me start with the property sheet. How many bedrooms?" Brandon asked.

Seth answered questions for what felt like the next hour. Brandon wanted to know everything about the property—from the size of the house to the materials used to build the barn. By the time Brandon closed his folder, Seth felt a little melancholic about selling his childhood home.

It not only held the memories of his childhood, but the memories he had of his parents as well. If it hadn't been for Penny breaking off their engagement, Seth would've returned home as soon as he had finished his apprenticeship.

That Sunday morning hadn't only destroyed the dreams he had for him and Penny, but it had ruined the dreams he had of turning his father's barn into a workshop one day.

And now he was going to sell it.

Guilt washed over him. Would his father wanted him to sell the homestead or return to it? Seth knew that was his father wanted no longer mattered, but it mattered to Seth.

"That's all from me. Now if you have questions, you can leave a message at my office. I'll be coming by to look at the property later today. Would that suit you?"

Seth nodded. "I'll be there."

Brandon left a few dollar bills on the table and bid farewell to Seth before he left the coffee shop. Seth rubbed his hands together, wishing he had a project that could help him tide over the time. All this sitting around and remembering the life he once had here was getting to him.

He turned his gaze towards the window and felt his heart skip a beat.

Outside on the sidewalk was the reason for his heartache and broken dreams. She hadn't aged a single day in the seven years since he'd seen her. In fact, if Seth was honest, she looked even prettier to him now.

Her skinny frame had softened just enough to make her more feminine. She still braided her hair beneath her prayer kapp and her smile still made his heart ache with longing. Or was it love?

Seth was helpless to look away. He couldn't drag his gaze from Penny as she talked to her husband.

He was holding a small boy and the hand of an older boy, while Penny held a little girl and a duplicate of the older boy's hand.

Twins, Seth thought with a smile. They had blessed penny with twins.

She smiled at something her husband said before she lowered herself to meet one twin in the eye. After talking to him for a few seconds, his face split in two with a smile.

It felt as if someone had just stabbed Seth in the heart with a dull blade. Envy washed over him like poison. Penny had everything he had dreamed of having with her.

Only she had it with someone else. Her husband seemed a year or two older than Seth. Even through the window of the coffee shop, Seth could see they shared a connection.

If he had thought he was ready to face the love of his past, Seth had been wrong.

Instead, he felt his world spin off its axis, unsure of where it was going to land. He had known that Penny would've moved on with her life. He just hadn't realized how much it would hurt to see her with her family.

He cleared his throat and dragged his gaze away from the window.

Even if the first offer on his father's homestead was from an Englisch couple, Seth wouldn't hesitate to accept it.

The sooner he put Lancaster County and Penny behind him, the better.

Chapter 7
Green Monsters

By the time Penny was done, her knees were aching.

Old Mrs. King had been hiring her once a month to clean her home ever since she had broken her hip two years before. Penny always enjoyed it when she went to work for Mrs. King. The widow would delight her tales of times gone past while offering Penny tea every hour.

To Penny, it felt more like a social visit with a few chores than a day's work.

But today it had felt like a week's work.

When she had scrubbed the wooden floors, Mrs. King had insisted it wasn't necessary. But Penny had wanted to the physical work to take her mind off Seth. Ever since his return to Lancaster County, and their small town in particular, she couldn't stop thinking of what might have been if she had made a different decision seven years ago.

Only when she had scrubbed a square of about a foot by a foot of the floor had she realized how dirty the wooden floors were. A job she had estimated wouldn't take her more than an hour at the most had taken her three hours to complete. Her shoulders were stiff, her elbows complaining from the backwards and forward motion and her knees felt as if she had crawled over gravel.

Why hadn't she thought to use a small pillow or an old towel to ease the burden on her knees?

It was too late now; she thought as she let out a heavy sigh.

Mrs. King had paid her extra for her trouble, but that didn't ease the long walk ahead for Penny. Mrs. King lived at least five miles from Penny's home. Usually, the walk was a lovely way to clear her mind and breathe in some fresh air, but today her body contested her with every single step.

As she walked, she remembered the long walks she and Seth took when they were courting. They would've walked for miles without realizing how far they had walked, simply captivated by each other's conversation.

But Penny didn't have any conversation today. Only her memories taunting her of how dull her life was. Seeing Seth again only made Penny painfully aware that she hadn't taken a single step forward in her life since the day she had bid him farewell.

She was still living with her parents, still single, and still didn't have a familye to care for. Her life had never felt emptier than it did now.

It might have been the exhaustion, the memories, or the feelings of failure, but Penny felt tears begin to well in her eyes as she reached halfway. She walked on the side of the road, turning her eyes up to the sky, hoping the fresh air would stop her from crying as the breeze kissed her cheeks.

But she tripped and the next moment she was rolling in the dirt, like a pig in a mud pen. A jolt of pain shot up her ankle towards her knee, making Penny reach for it instinctively.

Her ankle definitely wasn't broken, but she had twisted it badly.

The pain throbbed, although her ankle didn't look any worse for wear.

Without being able to stop them, the tears streamed over her cheeks.

Tears of regret.

Tears of pain.

Tears of longing.

Penny wasn't sure how long she lay on her side by the side of the road, clutching onto her ankle, but when she heard horse hooves come to a stop beside her, she quickly wiped the tears away.

"Penny?"

Penny cringed; she didn't have to turn her head to recognize that voice. She heard it every night in her dreams. It haunted her memories and now it was standing right beside her.

Could she have dreamed of a more terrible way for her and Seth to talk to each other again for the first time?

"Jah?" Penny asked, refusing to look at him. She was humiliated enough as it is.

"Are you alright?" Seth asked, moving around her and crouching beside her. He looked her over and saw the way she held her ankle. "Did you hurt your ankle?"

Penny sighed. "I think I twisted it slightly."

"What are you doing all the way out here?" Seth asked, glancing around as if to see who she was with.

"Walking home," Penny said curtly.

"Should I go get your husband? "Seth offered before he shook his head. "Nee, that will take too long. I'm not leaving you on the side of the road writhing in pain."

Penny frowned. Where did he want to find her husband? She didn't even have one?

"Kumm, put your arms around my neck and I'll help you up," Seth said with a kind tone of voice.

Penny shook her head. "I'll be fine. I'll be right as rain in a minute. I'm just waiting for the pain to ease. You can go on."

"I'm not going anywhere," Seth said firmly, crossing his arms. "Now either I can sit here with you until you feel better, or I can take you home so you can get some ice on that ankle. What is it going to be?"

Penny frowned at him. "When did you get so demanding?"

"Since you've always been stubborn," Seth retorted.

Penny couldn't stop her mouth from curving slightly. She has forgotten how fun it was to duel with Seth and she had forgotten how handsome he was.

She had forgotten how her heart seemed to float in her chest whenever he looked at her.

Penny cleared her throat and shrugged. "If you really want to go through all the trouble of taking me home, then fine."

"Fine," Seth said, lowering his neck enough for her to clasp her hands behind it.

He lifted her until she could stand on her foot, his hands on her hips as he set her on the ground.

It felt as if her skin had caught alight. Penny quickly stepped back, startled by the powerful reaction she still had for Seth Mast.

"Ouch!" Pain shot through her ankle the moment she stepped on it.

This time, Seth caught her just before she fell. Without even asking her permission, he scooped her up and carried her to his buggy. "I hope your mann will understand that these are extenuating circumstances."

Penny frowned, but before she could ask him what mann he was talking about, he moved around the buggy and climbed in. He took the reins and called to the horse. "Step up."

For a few moments, Penny allowed herself to really look at Seth. He had aged well; he had truly become even more handsome. Her heart yearned for them to be like they once were, but Penny knew Seth would never forgive her for breaking off their engagement.

She turned herself away from him when he turned to her with a question. "Where do you live?"

Penny frowned. "Where I've always lived."

"Gut, it won't take long before we're there. Are you comfortable?"

Penny couldn't help but chuckle. "Every muscle in body hurts, my ankle is throbbing, and I'm covered in dirt, but jah, I'm comfortable."

Seth offered her a crooked smile before he turned his eyes back onto the road.

Penny wondered if his wife would understand if she learned he'd carried her into his buggy and was now driving her home?

The mere thought of Seth's wife made her green with envy.

Chapter 8
Shattered Dreams

Seth stopped the buggy as close as he could to the porch steps. There was no one in sight in the yard and he wasn't sure it would be appropriate if Penny's husband caught him carrying her inside.

He climbed out of the buggy and was about to ask her where he could find her husband when the front door opened and Sarah Hershberger rushed onto the porch. "Penny? Did something happen?"

"Mamm…" Penny flinched when she tried to climb out of the buggy.

"Hullo Mrs. Hershberger. I found her lying on the side of the road. Looks like she took a real spill and twisted her ankle."

"Ach nee, you poor thing. Seth, help me get her out," Mrs. Hershberger said, as if he had been there courting her daughter just the day before.

As if seven years and a broken engagement had never even happened.

"I'm fine, Mamm, really. Seth, you really don't have to…" Penny argued as Seth reached for her. He ignored her complaints and scooped her up before he set her down on the ground, making sure she was close enough to the buggy for support.

"Here, let me help you," Mrs. Hershberger said, sliding an arm around Penny's waist. "Lean on me and hop on your gut foot."

Penny glanced over her shoulder and met Seth's gaze. He felt the same jolt of energy race through his body like he always did when she looked at him that way. Her smile was small, but her voice was grateful when she spoke. "Denke Seth."

"My pleasure," Seth said before clearing his throat. He couldn't allow himself to be vulnerable again. Penny had moved on and now had a family of her own; he had no place thinking of what he might have shared with her. "I'll just be on my way."

Seth didn't stay to make sure she was safely inside. He also didn't stay to meet her husband. After laying eyes on the man once, he couldn't help but feel a little judgmental.

Penny's parents had insisted they call off the engagement because Seth had nothing to offer her, no way to provide for her. Now she had married a man that looked more like a slight scarecrow than a farmer and they were living on her parents' property?

Why did her parents approve of him and not of Seth?

He couldn't help but feel offended. Perhaps being able to provide for Penny had never been the real issue at hand. Perhaps there had been something else.

Maybe the Hershbergers simply didn't like him. Or perhaps...

He tried to push the thought away, but it kept circling back until he allowed himself to consider it.

Perhaps Penny just didn't want to marry him and had used her parents as an excuse.

The thought was even too horrible to consider.

He pushed all thoughts of Penny from his mind, eager to get home. What he needed now was the mundaneness of chores, cooking and cleaning to occupy his mind until it was time for bed.

Hopefully tonight, he wouldn't dream of Penny again.

"Don't make jokes like that, Penny, you'll give me a heart attack."

In his dream, Seth was eighteen years old again. He was standing outside the barn where Penny would be baptized, excited to have the bishop announce their engagement afterward. Penny looked bright, just as bright as their future promised to be. In her eyes, he could see his whole life's happiness unfold before him.

But this morning it seemed as if there were storm clouds drifting in her gaze.

"I'm not making a joke," Penny said earnestly. "I'm breaking off our engagement."

"But... why would you do that? Yesterday you were happy about it, you said jah without even hesitating. What changed?" Seth asked, feeling as if someone had knocked the wind out of him.

"Everything," Penny sighed heavily. "We're too young, Seth. We still have our whole lives ahead of us. Don't you think we're rushing into things?"

"Nee. I know what my heart wants, Penny. My heart wants you. I don't want to go to Indiana and just leave you here, hoping you'll wait for me. I want you to come with, as my frau. I want you to join me on this adventure and when my apprenticeship is over, we'll come back here and start a new life together. A life with a familye," Seth tried to plead.

Penny's eyes were dry as she shook her head. "I'm not going to Indiana. I will not marry you."

"Penny, please. I don't understand what's going on?" Seth asked desperately.

"My parents won't give their blessing. They say you can't provide for me, you can't care for a familye, and you have nothing to your name. They won't let me give up me entire future on a whim. I can't go against them, Seth," Penny explained, emotion finally creeping into her voice.

"So your parents are forcing you to break up with me?" Seth asked, confused. "I thought they liked me?"

"They did, I mean they do. They just don't think we should get married," Penny explained.

"Penny, the apprenticeship can last for up to three years. I can't be away from you that long? Even if I come and visit, it won't be often. Please don't do this. I know you love me, I know you want to marry me. Why are you allowing them to ruin our lives?" Seth pleaded in a whisper as community members arrived for Sunday service.

"They're looking out for me, and I have to obey their wishes. I'm sorry, Seth. But it's over. Best of luck in Indiana." Penny turned her back on him and walked away.

Seth felt the blood drain from his face, even as his heart sank to soles of his feet. He had never felt so heavy or so *empty before. He watched Penny walk away and felt as if someone was tearing his heart into small little pieces. He tried to catch his breath, but his lungs simply wouldn't cooperate.*

Not knowing what else to do, he ran.

Not towards Penny, but away from her and all the reasons she couldn't marry him.

Seth woke up with a start. Cold sweat beaded his forehead even as he gasped for air. He hadn't dreamt of that day in so long, and it felt as if he has just relived it.

His hand rested over his racing heart and he wondered if it would ever be whole again?

Chapter 9
Unanswered Questions

"I'm grateful someone found you on the side of the road. I'm just not sure I like that it was him," Sarah said as soon as Penny was seated in the kitchen.

"I didn't exactly plan on falling, Mamm, otherwise I might have asked someone else to come and pick me up," Penny snapped a little harshly.

Her mother gave her a stern look, making it clear she would not allow herself to be sassed.

"I'm sorry, Mamm, it just hurts," Penny apologized as she lifted her ankle onto another chair.

"I can see that. It's swelling. Luckily it doesn't look too bad. You'll be back on your feet in no time. A day or two with it elevated and iced will work like a charm." Sarah returned with a bag of frozen peas and laid it over Penny's ankle.

"I thought he'd left already?"

Penny shrugged. "Me too."

Her mother let out a sigh, not revealing her feelings or her thoughts. For a moment, Penny wanted to ask her mother if she regretted standing by her father's decision all those years ago. But she was simply in too much pain and too exhausted to even consider broaching the subject.

Instead, she let out a sigh and shook her head. "This was one of the worst days. I scrubbed Mrs. King's floors until my arms and my knees hurt and then I fell on my way home."

"My poor dochder, you shouldn't work so hard. Mrs. King will surely understand if you only scrub a section of the floor at a time. To do it all at once, along with the laundry, the dusting, and changing the linens... it's too much for one day."

"I know, Mamm, but I offered. I just didn't realize how long I would scrub until I started."

"I'll make you a gut strong cup of tea and fetch you something for the pain. How about that?" Sarah offered kindly.

"Denke Mamm," Penny said before her mother disappeared down the hallway.

On her own for a moment, she couldn't help but wonder if fate was playing tricks on her. Why did it have to Seth to help her, and why did her mother have to pretend as if he didn't belong in their community?

More so, why did Seth keep referring to her husband?

She thought of Mary Yoder and wondered if her loose tongue had taken her gossip a little too far before she quickly prayed for forgiveness. Mary Yoder might be a lot of things, but she wasn't a liar.

Which begged the question: why did Seth think she was married?

A sigh escaped her, realizing he probably accepted she was married because he had a wife in Indiana.

Penny couldn't help but wonder what she looked like, what her personality was like, and if she loved Seth as much as Penny once did.

"Here you go, two pain tablets, and the tea is coming right up. Is that ice helping?" Sarah asked as she set the tablets down in front of Penny.

Penny had completely forgotten about her ankle for a moment. "It's uh… it's already feeling better."

"Gut girl. Now, once you've had your tea, go lie down on the sofa and keep that ankle elevated, you hear?"

"Jah Mamm." Penny smiled at her mother. Although she was a grown woman, whenever she hurt herself, her mother still treated her as if she was four years old.

She thought of Seth and couldn't imagine losing her own parents.

A wave of guilt rushed over her as she realized she hadn't even offered him sympathies for the passing of his father. She'd remember next time, she promised herself.

Almost as soon as she made the promise, she pushed the thought aside.

There wouldn't be a next time. Seth was probably eager to return home to his family and didn't even think twice about Penny or her condolences.

To him, she was nothing but a person from his past.

The only problem was, for Penny, Seth was still very much present in her heart.

Chapter 10
An Unexpected Visitor

Regardless of his decision to accept the first offer he received on his father's property; Seth turned it down.

Brandon Williams had stopped by this morning with an Englisch couple that viewed the homestead. They didn't mind that there were some repairs to be done on the house and the fences, or that the barn roof was leaking. The couple were looking for a simpler life and for them, that meant buying Seth's childhood home.

When Brandon had handed him the offer to purchase, Seth had simply shaken his head.

He couldn't explain it to the Englisch realtor or the Englisch couple, but it just didn't feel right. Perhaps it wasn't the right people, or perhaps he just wasn't ready to let go of his father's legacy just yet.

For the rest of the day, Seth had busied himself with small repairs around the house. With every problem he found, he couldn't help but feel guilty for not visiting his father over the last seven years. The repairs weren't large, but rather small, menial tasks that his father wasn't up to doing anymore.

The more Seth worked, the more he wondered if selling would be the right decision. Perhaps instead of selling the property he should only put it up for lease.

He pushed the thought aside as soon as it came to mind. As long as he owned property in Lancaster County, there would be an invisible string tying him to the place he wanted to forget.

Because that invisible string would always bring him back to Penny.

Yesterday, when he'd seen her on the side of the road, his heart had simply stopped. Just the thought of her being hurt had upset him so much that he hadn't even bothered with propriety when he had picked her up without her permission.

He was expecting her husband to come knocking at any moment to chasten him for his behavior. Although Mrs. Hershberger had seemed grateful that he'd rescued Penny, he knew she didn't like him very much. Why else would she have refused for Penny to marry him?

If anyone was going to run to Penny's husband about Seth driving her home, it would be Mrs. Hershberger.

For that reason, Seth wasn't even surprised when there was a knock on his front door late in the afternoon. Knowing who it was and what he was there for, Seth took his time before he answered the door. He was ready to apologize and explain at the same time as he opened the door.

But instead of Penny's husband, it was Mary Yoder beaming at him with a smile a mile wide and a basket filled with baked goods.

"Mary? Mary Yoder?" Seth asked, surprised and confused at the same time.

"I was wondering if you'd remember my name. Here's a little something to welcome you back." Mary held out the basket and, without invitation, stepped past Seth into the house.

Seth sighed as he closed the door, wondering what Mary Yoder would want to visit him for.

"Denke, this is very kind of you. But I'm not staying. I'm just dealing with my daed's affairs and selling the property. As soon as that's done, I'm heading back to Indiana."

"Really? And what is it you do in Indiana?" Mary asked, taking a seat in the living room. "I wouldn't mind a glass of milk; it was quite a walk from my haus to here."

Seth was a little irritated by her forwardness, that and the way she kept flapping her lashes as if she had something in her eye. He set down the basket in the kitchen before pouring her a glass of milk.

"Here you go," Seth said, taking a seat on the edge of the sofa. Not intending to allow Mary to get too comfortable at all.

"Denke." Mary flashed him a beaming smile. "It's so gut to see you again."

Realizing what was happening, Seth quickly changed the subject. Mary Yoder had always been a gossip and a bit of a flirt with men. The last person he wanted her to turn her attention to was him.

"Carpentry. I have my workshop and do commissions in Indiana," Seth quickly explained.

"Really, you must make quite the living, then?" Mary probed even further.

"I do well enough. And what is it you do these days?" Seth returned the question.

Mary laughed. "Seth, don't be ridiculous. I don't work, if that's what you mean."

"Oh." Seth nodded, not surprised in the least. Mary had always been spoilt. Knowing that Mary had one talent, Seth tapped into it. "So what's news around here since I've been gone? Who got married, had kids?"

Mary began by giving him a rundown of almost every birth, funeral, and wedding that had taken place since he had left. Seth tried his best not to yawn with boredom, but he really wasn't interested in Abel's second daughter or Miriam's aunt that caused a scandal by falling pregnant out of wedlock after her husband passed.

"What about...Penny?" Seth tried not to make his specific interest evident to Mary.

Mary's laughter careened through the room. "What about her? You know she's only good enough to sew and clean?"

Seth clenched his jaw at the condescending way in which Mary spoke of Penny. Tired of her visit and her gossip, he stood up with an apologetic smile. "It was great catching up, Mary, but I really have quite a few things I still need to do today."

"Ach, that's a shame. I thought we might visit a little longer." Mary looked thoroughly disappointed.

"My apologies and once again, denke for the baked goods," Seth said, showing her to the door.

Once Mary was gone, Seth bit into a fresh bun and wondered what Mary had meant by Penny cleaning and sewing.

Was that all she did all day? Sewed clothes for her familye and cleaned after them?

Why was it that the thought bothered him?

Perhaps because it was what mothers did and Seth was jealous because she wasn't the mother of his children?

He pushed the thought aside and grabbed another roll before he headed outside. He'd fix a fence or hammer a shingle, anything to get his mind off Penny Hershberger.

Chapter 11
Admirable Advice

"It's gut to see you've all recovered from your ailments." Penny smiled as she took a seat at Anna's kitchen table.

Anna laughed. "Denke Gott. It's bad enough to feel ill, but to feel ill when you need to take care of four ill kinner and a mann… let's just say I prayed for a lot of strength and even more patience."

Penny couldn't help but laugh. "You should've told me you needed help."

"You helped enough by going to town with John. Denke, again." Anna sat down at the table and handed Penny her mug of tea. "So what gives me the pleasure of a visit this afternoon? Usually you're up to your ears in sewing this time of year."

"It's a little slower this year. The regular cleaning jobs are helping, but to be honest, I am a little concerned. My familye depends on the income I provide," Penny admitted. She wouldn't reveal to her parents that she was concerned about her income, but she could to her closest friend.

"I'll spread the word a bit about your sewing services. Perhaps people just need to be reminded that's its more affordable to have clothes made than to buy at the Mennonite outlet in town."

Penny nodded. Ever since the Mennonite clothing outlet opened in town, more and more Amish women were purchasing their prayer kapps, aprons, and husbands' vests there. Penny hadn't really felt it affect her business until the last few weeks.

"Denke, Anna. I'd appreciate it. In the meantime, I'll try to visit more often." Penny stared into her tea as she kept stirring it, lost in thought.

"Why do I have a feeling that money isn't the only thing on your mind? John says that Seth is back in town?" Anna asked with a cocked brow. "Have you seen him yet?"

Penny sighed heavily. "Jah, under the worst circumstances. I sprained my ankle a few days ago and none other than Seth Mast himself turned up at that very moment to find me in tears."

"Ach nee, I'm so sorry. You must have been so surprised?"

"I was. And then he scooped me up like an errant child and deposited me in his buggy." Penny laughed. "I don't know what was worse. To ride in a buggy with Seth again, or the way my mamm treated him. What's that saying? Kindness kills? She was kind enough to frighten away a snake."

"Oh, dear." Anna shrugged. "I guess Seth's return affects not only you. Do you think they regret having you break off the engagement?"

"I doubt it. To them, Seth will always be the mann that wasn't gut enough for their dochder," Penny admitted with a shrug.

"And to you, he was the only man that was gut enough? He's the reason you haven't courted again, isn't he?" Anna prodded gently.

Penny didn't want to reveal her innermost fears and doubts, but perhaps now that Seth was back it was time to be honest about how their broken engagement had affected her. "I don't know… I just think…I've never felt that way again, Anna. I fear that I never will."

Anna reached for her hand and squeezed it tightly. "You will, I promise. Seth left so soon after… perhaps you need to talk to him. To get closure for what happened in the past. You need to move on, Penny. You can't spend the rest of your life longing for what could've been."

"Why not? It's been so much fun," Penny said with a wry smile. "Besides, he's probably married to a beautiful frau with a house full of kinner. Talking to him now about the past would be humiliating. I don't want him to think that I've been pining for him all these years."

"You weren't pining, you merely haven't moved on," Anna pointed out.

"I have moved on, not out perhaps, but I have moved on," Penny argued.

"How exactly? You don't attend singings, you haven't been on another buggy ride, you don't entertain any mann that shows an interest in you. Penny, I'm saying this as a friend and because I love you. You deserve a future filled with love and light. You deserve to become a mamm and a frau, and none of that is going to happen unless you don't put Seth and what you shared with him behind you," Anna said with urgency.

Penny shook her head. "Anna, it is behind me."

"Really? Can you honestly tell me that seeing him again, riding in a buggy with him again, didn't upset you in the least?" Anna dared Penny to answer.

Penny let out a heavy sigh. "Fine, I'll admit I was a little shaken. But I'm fine, really. Besides, he'll be leaving soon, then I can forget about him for gut."

Anna laughed and shook her head as she squeezed Penny's hand. "But you and I both know that you'll never really completely forget about Seth or the dreams you shared."

"Can we focus on the tea or your kinner, or anything else than Seth Mast, please?" Penny all but pleaded.

Anna nodded. "Alright, I'll let it go. But remember, closure."

Penny rolled her eyes. She wasn't even sure what closure really meant. Was she supposed to discuss her parents' decision that changed her life irrevocably with a man that had already moved on?

Perhaps closure wasn't what she needed. What she needed was to steer clear of Seth until he returned to Indiana.

Chapter 12
Irony Can Be Humbling

Ever since the harvest, Penny had noticed her father seemed a little down.

She hadn't had the courage to ask him, because she knew that a poor harvest was her father's worst fear. But now that her sewing jobs were becoming less and less, she couldn't help but feel the urge to find more cleaning work to supplement her family's income.

After her visit with Anna yesterday, she was determined to forget about Seth Mast and instead focus on finding more work. She had spent the day catching up with all the chores at home, so that if a cleaning job became available, she wouldn't feel as if she were leaving her mother in a pinch.

Penny and her parents took their seats at the dinner table. A rich stew just waiting to be enjoyed was exactly what Penny needed after a busy day.

Everyone bowed their heads in silent prayer before they helped themselves to the stew. Neither her mother nor her father spoke a single word over dinner. It was as if a weight hung over the table, a dark cloud stifling them, almost.

"Mamm, Daed… is something wrong?" Penny asked once she had finished eating.

Her father glanced at her mother before he finally let out a heavy sigh. "I didn't want to bother you with this, but perhaps it's best you know."

"Know what, Daed?" Penny asked, concerned.

"The harvest…" her mother trailed off. "It wasn't what we were hoping for. We made enough to get by until next year, but just barely."

"I went to the bank today to see if I could secure a loan to see us through… but we don't have enough collateral," her father explained.

"We never meant to depend on your income, Penny, but right now we don't really have any other choice," her mother admitted quietly.

Penny could see how hard this was for her father. She glanced at her mother and back to her father. "Of course you should depend on my income. I'm twenty-four years old, Daed. You can't care for me forever. I'd like to help any way I can. I know the sewing has been down, but I'll find more cleaning jobs," Penny quickly promised.

"Denke Penny, we appreciate it. We'll just cut down our expenses for now. I'm sure we'll manage. Gott has always blessed us at the right time. I'm sure he'll bless us now again," her mother said with a hopeful smile.

"Actually…" her father trailed off. "The bishop told me about a cleaning job. I wasn't sure you'd be interested. But the pay is double your usual wages and right now we really need the money."

"What does the job entail if they're willing to pay double?" Penny asked curiously.

"They'd like to hire you permanently. It would be cleaning, packing, and many chores. Of course, if you don't want to, your mamm and I will make another plan," her father quickly added.

Penny shook her head. "I'll do it, Daed. I don't mind working hard and, like you said, the money would help a lot. Where is it? Who is it for?"

Her father glanced at her mother and her mother let out a heavy sigh.

"An Englischer?" Penny asked hesitantly. Her parents understood she preferred to work in their own community.

"Nee. It's for Seth Mast," her father finally revealed.

Penny's heart skipped a beat at the mention of Seth's name. "Seth? But I thought he was going back to Indiana?"

"He is, according to the bishop. The house is up for sale, but Seth needs someone to help him pack and clean the place thoroughly before he leaves for Indiana."

Penny's gaze darted from her mother to her father, and she couldn't help but feel a strange irony in the situation. All those years ago, her parents had insisted that Seth wasn't good enough to become her husband, but now his money was good enough to help them out of a bind. "I'm not sure..."

"Penny, please. What happened between the two of you is in the past. We really, really, need the money," her mother all but pleaded.

Penny could see the desperation on her father's face and knew that his was one of the hardest things he'd ever had to ask her.

Finally, she nodded. "Okay, I'll do it."

Chapter 13
Thou Shalt Not Covet

There hadn't been another offer on his father's property, but when the next offer came, Seth wanted to be ready.

After seeing Penny and having Mary almost throwing herself at him, Seth couldn't help but realize it was time to go back to Indiana. It was time to forget about Penny and her perfect family and escape the memories of the past.

The bishop had stopped by the day before to come and see how Seth was holding up. When Seth had mentioned that he wanted to sort through his father's things to keep what he wanted and donate the rest to charity, the bishop had agreed it was a good way to find closure. While he was at it, Seth wanted to make sure the house was clean and ready for the new owners to move in once he found someone who wanted to buy the property.

But to get everything done in record time, he would need help.

The bishop had kindly offered to send someone his way. Someone who was a magician at cleaning and a whiz with sorting. A magician and a whiz were exactly what Seth needed now. He'd even pay double wages if the person could start today.

So with his coffee in his hand, he stood on the porch and watched the sun rise in the East. He couldn't help but feel melancholic, wondering how many more sunrises he would have the privilege of watching in Lancaster County before he left for good.

What confused him even more was why he had never felt the same connection with Indiana that he felt here.

This was where all his fondest memories were. The memories of his childhood, his father, and, of course, his memories of Penny.

He pushed her far from his mind, reminding himself that to covet was a sin. He had already wasted enough years pining for her and wishing things could have been different. It was time for him to move on. Penny had looked happy when he'd seen her in town. She had a whole brood of children and although her husband didn't seem to suit her; they seemed to get along well.

Penny was no longer his concern, and the sooner he left, the sooner he would remember that.

Once he had finished his first cup of coffee, he headed inside. After grabbing another cup of coffee, he headed to his father's room to begin. He opened the closet and saw all his father's clothes hanging there. His heart ached with grief and loss.

He hadn't realized how hard it was going to be to pack away his father's things. Although the funeral had already been held, it felt as if Seth was about to put away his father, this time in a more permanent sense. There wouldn't be any reminders that his father had once lived here when Seth left for Indiana.

The thought saddened him more than he had realized.

For the second time, he had doubts about selling the property. He knew it was for the best. He couldn't just give up his life in Indiana and move back here only to face what he could never have.

Penny.

Seth pushed through the pain and grief and removed the clothes from the closet. He laid everything out on the bed, knowing that they would donate them to charity. Or perhaps he should give them to the bishop; the bishop would know who in the community could do with clothes that were still in a good condition.

A smile curved his mouth as he held up his father's forgut suit. Seth knew it wouldn't fit him, but he didn't have the heart to put it on the donation pile. Instead, he hung it in front of the closet. He would take it with him. Perhaps one day he could give it to his son.

Seth didn't keep track of the time as he worked. He didn't even bother with breakfast, instead, he continued to pack up his father's room. Although the bishop had promised that help would come today, Seth couldn't help but feel that this was a private chore.

One he needed to do, one that would help him grieve his loss.

He sat down on the side of the bed and reached for his father's bible. He smiled sadly, remembering all the times he'd father had read to him from that very bible when he was young. Seth had learned right from wrong through the stories in that bible. He'd learned the Lord's word and what his expectations were for his followers.

He couldn't help but wonder what the Lord's expectations were of him now. Did the Lord approve of him letting go of his father's house? Did the Lord approve of his idea of returning to Indiana and never to return?

Did the Lord approve of Penny's husband?

The question caught him off guard even as he heard a knock on the front door. Seth set down the bible and headed to the door to welcome the person the bishop had sent. As he opened the door, his breath caught even as his heart skipped a beat.

Wasn't the plan to avoid Penny at all costs? Then why was she standing on his porch holding a bucket and wearing a hesitant smile?

"Penny?" Seth asked, confused.

Penny shrugged. "Seth, you needed someone to help you clean and pack."

"The bishop sent you?"

Penny shook her head. "Nee. I mean jah, indirectly. He told my daed, he signed me up for the job. If you'd rather I leave…"

Seth paused for a moment, stuck between the past and the present. There was a time he wouldn't have hesitated to invite Penny into his home, but now…

He shrugged and summoned a smile. "Nee, please. I really need your help. Besides, the bishop said you're the best."

Penny's laughter made his blood warm even as it brought the familiar joy to Seth's heart. "I'm sure he was over-exaggerating."

Chapter 14
Incorrect Presumptions

Penny could see that it was just as awkward for Seth to have her there as it was for her to be there. On her way to Seth's home, she had been tempted countless times to just turn back and go home.

She couldn't imagine that he would want her in his house, or that his wife would be pleased to hear about her presence. But then, Seth probably hadn't even bothered to tell his wife about her, or their shared past. To Seth, she was the past.

"Would you like to come inside?" Seth asked after a few moments.

Penny nodded, feeling foolish as she picked up her bucket with cleaning supplies. She couldn't believe how the fates had turned. All those years ago he hadn't been good enough and now here she was cleaning his home because her father needed the money.

She stopped right inside the door, unsure what to do next.

Seth dragged a hand through his hair. "I uhm... how about some kaffe?"

Penny wasn't thirsty, but she could tell that Seth needed a moment to process her presence. "Sure, denke."

She followed him into the kitchen, remembering how much time she had spent there in the past. Only this time, everything was different.

Seth poured them each a cup of kaffe and without asking, added one spoon of sugar and cream for her. Only when he set the cup down in front of her, did he realize what he had done.

"I'm sorry, I didn't even ask..." Seth shook his head.

"It's alright, you got it right." Penny smiled, surprised that he'd remembered after all these years.

Seth sighed and let out a nervous chuckle. "Is it supposed to be this awkward?"

Penny couldn't help but laugh. "I do not know."

"Me neither." Seth shrugged.

"Then let's make it easier. Where would you like me to start?" Penny asked meeting his gaze.

Seth was still the most handsome man she'd ever met. Or perhaps he was only handsome to her because her heart seemed to race whenever he was near.

Seth's eyes widened. "I uhm... I hadn't really thought it through. I just... I'm selling the place, so I need to clear out Daed's things and get it cleaned. I started in his room..." Seth trailed off.

Penny didn't need to hear the rest of the sentence to understand. His father's room was something Seth needed to do on his own. "Why don't I start in the other bedroom? I can start by clearing out the closet, then you can go through everything while I clean."

"Gut idea," Seth agreed. "Do you need anything?"

Penny frowned with a crooked smile. "To unpack a closet? I think my hands will do."

Seth chuckled. "Right. Call me if you need me."

For the next few hours, Penny was all alone in the second bedroom. She unpacked everything from spare linens, quilts, extra cleaning supplies and even old clothes onto the bed. When she was done unpacking the closet, she set about washing the curtains. She wasn't sure if Seth was going to take them or leave them, but either way, they would at least be clean.

She was just about to go and find him when he found her by the washing line. "You didn't have to wash those."

"They needed it," Penny said with a shrug as she placed the last peg.

"And you need lunch. Come on." Seth turned and headed to the house.

Penny followed him, surprised that he had been thoughtful enough to make her lunch. As soon as she walked into the kitchen, her heart swelled in her chest. Just like Seth had remembered how she liked her coffee, he had remembered her weakness for tomato, ham, and cheese sandwiches.

Or perhaps it was a coincidence, she reminded herself.

"I didn't know what else to make, but I remember you used to like these," Seth confirmed her suspicions.

"I still do, denke. You don't have to cater to me, Seth. I brought a sandwich," Penny said, sitting down at the table.

"Tomorrow you don't have to. While you're helping me, I'll make sure you're fed and watered." Seth laughed. "I know, you're not a horse."

Penny couldn't help but join with laughter. Nothing had ever been awkward between her and Seth and ever since she had seen him on the side of the road a week ago, it had been nothing but.

"How's your ankle doing? Seems it recovered with little trouble?" Seth asked.

Penny nodded. "Right as rain, thanks to frozen peas."

"Gut to hear. I'm sure your husband must have been very concerned," Seth said with a searching look.

Penny set down her sandwich and met his gaze with a curious look of her own. "Why would you think I have one?"

"I saw you and your familye in town the other day. You have beautiful kinner, Penny," Seth said almost heavily.

Penny was confused for a moment before it dawned on her. Laughter bubbled from her throat before she shook her head. "Seth, that wasn't my familye. It was Anna's. She was sick and asked me to accompany her husband to town to take the twins to the doctor. I don't have a husband."

Seth's frown deepened even more. "So you're not married?"

"Nee," Penny shook her head. Why did admitting that make her feel less somehow?

Seth's expression changed to one of curiosity. "Engaged?"

"Nee," Penny admitted again.

She didn't want Seth to think she had spent all these years pining for him, but she couldn't lie, either. "And before you ask, nee I'm not being courted."

Seth shook his head, looking confused. "Why not?"

Penny chuckled. "Because… no one has asked to court me."

"But Penny, you're such a wunderbaar woman. You're kind, generous, and loving. Don't the men in Lancaster County see that?" Seth asked, baffled that she was still single.

Penny shrugged. She wouldn't dare reveal to him she had avoided every offer of courtship since he left. She also wouldn't tell him she hadn't been attending singings for the same reasons she had turned down offers of courtship.

For Penny, there had always only been Seth, and seeing him again now only brought back all the memories of how wonderful they had been together.

But she couldn't allow herself to get lost in the past. Seth had a wife, a family, and an entire life in Indiana that didn't include her.

Just the thought of Seth's wife made her blood turn green. She didn't want to be a witness to everything Seth had without her, but she wished she could just whisper into Seth's wife's ear how lucky she was to have Seth in her life.

Perhaps Anna had been right, Penny needed to find closure. Maybe working for him for the next few days would help her make peace with the fact that Seth had moved on.

But if she could move on? That was another question entirely.

Chapter 15
A Moment in Time

"How about you?" Penny asked after a moment.

Seth was still reeling after learning that Penny wasn't married. When he had returned to Lancaster County, he had held no hope of reconnecting with Penny. But now, it was as if hope had bloomed in his chest.

After spending the last few years thinking of her and longing for the future they didn't have, he couldn't help but feel as if he might get a second chance to win over Penny's heart. This time, she was old enough to make her own decisions.

But then, there were her parents.

Her parents had forced her to break off their engagement—would they still object if Seth managed by some miracle to make Penny fall in love with him again?

"Seth?" Penny asked, drawing him back into the moment.

Seth smiled and shook his head. "Sorry, I didn't hear you?"

Penny nodded. Her eyes had shadows in them as she spoke. "And you? How many kinner do you have?"

Seth frowned, confused. "Kinner?"

"Ach, I'm sorry, are your kinner still boppli?" Penny quickly rephrased her question.

Seth wasn't sure if he had missed out on a part of the conversation, but Penny's questions simply made little sense to him at all. "Penny, I'm sorry, but I really don't understand."

Penny sighed heavily. "Your kinner, Seth. How old are they? Your frau must be a saint for taking care of them while you're here taking care of your daed's affairs."

Seth chuckled, realizing she had made the same wrong assumptions about him. Seth couldn't help but be pleased to see the shadows in her gaze. Did it mean that she still had feelings for him, like he did for her? "Penny, I tried courting when I arrived in Indiana. I soon learned that no one was you. I haven't courted in five years. I'm not married, and I don't have any kinner, boppli or otherwise."

Penny's eyes widened with surprise. "You're not… you don't…" she trailed off.

Seth nodded as the shadows in her eyes faded. "Instead of trying to find someone to spend my life with, I made carpentry my life."

"You must enjoy it then," Penny commented a little strangely. Clearly, she was just as surprised by his revelations as he had been about hers.

"I do. Just like the bishop tells me you enjoy cleaning and sewing if I remember correctly?"

Penny nodded. "The sewing I've always enjoyed. The cleaning just happened. Someone asked for my help one day and before I knew it I kept going back, only they paid me. Word spread somehow."

"For who do you clean? Englischers?" Seth asked curiously.

Penny shrugged. "Mostly elderly folk in the community that can't manage on their own anymore. I haven't ever worked for Englischers. I don't know why, but I prefer remaining in the community than to seek work outside of it."

"Staying close to your beliefs is always wise," Seth agreed. "And the sewing?"

"Ach, you know, dresses, aprons, prayer kapps, vests, coats… the usual. But the sewing has really trickled down since the Mennonite outlet opened in town. And with Daed's harvest, I could really have used the sewing income."

"Your father's harvest?" Seth asked with a frown.

"We had late hail and some of the crop was damaged. Daed only sold about half our usual crops," Penny admitted wryly.

"I'm so sorry to hear that Penny. It must be very hard for your daed."

"It is. That's why I was so grateful for the extra cleaning job here," Penny admitted with a sad smile. "Although I must admit, I wasn't keen to work for you."

Seth laughed. "Why on earth wouldn't you want to work for me?"

"I wasn't sure if it would be awkward… after all this time."

"It was this morning," Seth admitted.

Penny chuckled. "You're right, it was."

"I'm glad we talked, Penny," Seth said, his smile fading. He searched her gaze for something; anything that would reveal to him if she still cared about him.

Her gaze softened. "Me too. I better get going. You're not paying me for my conversation."

Penny stood up, but Seth wasn't ready to let her go just yet. He reached for her wrist as she moved past him. Penny stopped and turned to him with a questioning look. "I would pay even more for your conversation and your company, Penny."

Their gazes met and held, and it was as if they were back at that afternoon when he'd asked for her hand in marriage.

Seth felt his heart swell with hope, relieved that she hadn't moved on. If he was honest, he had been in a hurry to leave Lancaster County because he couldn't stand to meet Penny's husband and see what a happy life she had without him.

But now, everything had changed.

Penny was still available, and so was he.

The air thickened between them with emotions from long ago. Neither willing to let go or to move on. Seth felt his mouth curve and saw her mouth curve in response.

"I'm glad we talked, Penny," Seth said in a quiet voice.

Penny nodded. "I'm glad we talked too."

He held her gaze for another moment before he let her go. Alone in the kitchen, Seth looked around, searching for answers.

Did Gott bring him back to learn Penny was still alone? Or did he bring him back to get over Penny and finally move on?

Seth closed his eyes and murmured a quiet prayer for the Lord to lead him on the path he had chosen for him. When he stood up to continue cleaning out his father's room, he glanced into the spare bedroom and caught sight of Penny. His heart swelled with renewed interest for the girl he had never forgotten.

Chapter 16
Vultures and Their Prey

Penny sat beside her mother in the barn while the deacon delivered his sermon. Sunday Service was the highlight of Penny's week. Listening to Gott's word gave her a chance to reflect on her actions of the two weeks before and to learn from her mistakes.

It also gave her the opportunity to make wise decisions about how she wanted to follow in the Lord's footsteps and how she could better live a life of consequence and example.

But today she couldn't seem to focus on the deacon's words. She only realized she was fidgeting when her mother touched her hand with a curious look.

It had been two days since she and Seth had shared a moment in his kitchen. She had spent most of yesterday reliving the moment and trying to figure out what it had meant. As she sat in the barn where the church service was being held today, she couldn't help but feel a little anxious about what tomorrow would bring.

Would Seth be distant and quiet like he had been on the day he had helped her with her ankle, or would he be the same man she had fallen in love with all those years ago?

Like he had been when she had shared lunch with him in his kitchen on Friday?

All these years she had believed that Seth had moved on and begun a new life in Indiana. Learning now that he had never married, had no children, and hadn't even bothered to court over the last five years, awakened many feelings inside.

Most of all regret.

Because not only had she wasted all these years regretting the decision to break off their engagement, but it seemed Seth had also lost years of his life due to the decision that had been made for her.

Penny glanced towards the men and spotted her father sitting near the front. She couldn't harbor anger for her father over what he had done, but she could blame him for the way his actions had affected Seth's life.

Her father had been wrong, and realizing that now hurt more than it did all those years ago. Penny asked herself the same question repeatedly.

Should she have gone against her father's wishes?

Penny sighed quietly as the service ended. Even now, she still couldn't imagine going against her father's wishes. But she wondered if her father had ever considered the consequences of what he had done.

"Penny, kumm," her mother coaxed Penny from her thoughts. "Service is over."

Penny didn't even realize the congregation had moved outside to the table of refreshments. She followed her mother mindlessly, still lost somewhere in the past and Friday afternoon.

She poured herself a glass of lemonade and went to say hello to Anna and her familye. A smile curved her mouth as she joined them. Anna was truly blessed with a beautiful family. When Anna had told Penny of her engagement to John, Penny had been doubtful at first. Until he had and Anna had courted, Penny had always thought John to be quiet and withdrawn, shy even.

But just like John had brought her friend happiness and love, Anna had brought him to life. John was a wonderful father and a kind husband, exactly what Anna deserved.

"I heard you have a new cleaning job?" Anna asked, cocking a brow before she nodded towards where Seth was standing talking to one of his friends from childhood.

Penny shrugged. "Jah. Cleaning and clearing out his daed's things."

"I see. Have you asked about his frau?" Anna asked curiously.

Penny couldn't stop the smile from splitting her face in two. "He doesn't have one."

"What?" Anna asked, surprised. "Penny, that's..." Anna's entire expression changed as she let out a heavy sigh. "Apparently, Mary learned that as well."

Penny turned to see Mary Yoder laughing at something Seth said. Even from a distance, it was clear Mary was making her interest in Seth no secret.

A stab of envy punched through Penny's stomach as she watched Seth smile at Mary.

Any brief flicker of hope that had sparked after the moment they had shared on Friday evaporated as she watched Mary all but throw herself at Seth, and Seth seeming to enjoy the attention.

"Have a blessed Sunday, Anna. I've got to get going. My parents will want to leave soon."

Anna frowned, but nodded. "You too."

Penny didn't waste any time to find her parents. "I'm ready to leave if you are."

Her mother nodded. "Jah, best we get going to get lunch on the table."

Penny waited while her mother fetched her father from where he was talking with a group of elders. Her gaze, as if drawn to him by an invisible string, travelled towards Seth again.

Mary was still standing by his side, fluttering her eyelashes and smiling at him with hope and flattery.

Seth caught sight of Penny over Mary's shoulder. He looked right at her, like he had done all those years ago. He looked at her as if he could see right into her heart. As if nothing else in the world mattered.

Penny felt a light blush color her skin as the past came rushing back again.

When he broke their gaze and turned to smile at Mary, Penny realized she had probably imagined it. Seth might not have moved on, but clearly Mary appealed to him.

Why else would he smile at her?

With a heavy heart and a mind filled with unanswered questions, Penny followed her parents to the buggy.

Chapter 17
A Cross Road

Seth was deaf to Mary's mindless chattering.

Just like when she had showed up at his house, her attention was unwanted and unexpected. He watched Penny follow her parents back to the buggy. With a longing gaze, he wished he had answers to all the questions circling his mind.

Learning that Penny was still free, just as he was, had been a welcome surprise. It was as if the years in between had never happened at all. The feelings he had for her back then were still strong as ever. His heart still skipped a beat at the sight of her, and his blood pumped happily through his veins whenever he noticed her smile.

Whatever had drawn him to Penny all those years ago was even stronger now.

But that confused Seth more than anything else.

Because seven years ago he hadn't been good enough for her, what made him think he was worthy of her now?

"Seth? Did you hear what I just said?" Mary asked, touching his shoulder.

Seth turned to Mary with a polite but distant smile. "I'm sorry, Mary, my mind is rambling about everything I still need to do before I return to Indiana."

Mary's hopeful smile faded. "So you're not staying?"

Seth had made no decisions about staying and he knew in his heart there would only be one reason he wouldn't return to Indiana, and that was Penny.

"Nee, I need to get back. If you'll excuse me, I have to get home to continue packing." Seth turned and walked away from Mary.

He knew he had just been undoubtedly rude, but she wouldn't give him peace otherwise.

He took the reins and called to his horse. As soon as the horse moved, Seth wondered whether he should try to court Penny again. Should he pursue the feelings he still had for her, or was it time to put Penny in his past and move on?

Did the Lord bring him back to Lancaster County because of Penny?

Seth let out a heavy sigh. He wanted nothing more than to explore the feelings he still had for Penny, but the thought of being turned away a second time made him hesitant.

From the look in her eyes, it had been clear Penny still had feelings for him. But that didn't mean she wanted to pursue them. Perhaps it had just been a melancholic moment they had shared in his kitchen, but if it was more, didn't he owe it to himself to find out?

When he stopped the buggy in front of his barn, Seth found himself even more confused than before.

He stood at a crossroads, and the direction in which he turned would determine his future.

Did he return to Indiana and pursue his life there? Would he find someone he could love and have a family with?

Or did he give up his life in Indiana, and return to Lancaster County to pursue to love of his life?

He looked at his father's house, his childhood home, and wondered if he should sell it or wait for a short while longer until he had more clarity about which direction he wanted to turn.

Knowing that he was struggling to find the answers he needed, Seth turned his gaze to the blue sky.

"Gott, please hear my prayer. Help me understand the feelings I still have for Penny. Help me understand if they mean more than just a memory from the past. Seeing her again reminded me how much I care for her. Spending time with her reminds me of the future we had planned together.

Dear Gott, please help me. Give me a sign, or at least a nudge in the direction you have chosen for me. I beg you, Gott, lead me towards the future that will prosper me. And if that future is with Penny, Gott, please open her heart and her mind to the possibility of us reuniting. Ease her father's concerns and help him see me for the man that I am, the man that I have become. I beg of you, Gott. Amen."

Seth unhitched the horse and returned the buggy to its place before he headed inside.

Why was it that his home felt empty without Penny there?

She had only spent one day helping him and yet he already missed her presence. Seth had never felt lonely in his father's home before, but today he felt alone and fearful of what a future without Penny might hold.

Chapter 18
The Heart Has a Voice

"Penny, you are a lifesaver. I swear if Rebecca loses another prayer kapp, I might just shun her myself."

Relief shone on Anna's face as Penny handed her the prayer kapp at the door. "Don't be so dramatic. You know she doesn't have to wear one just yet."

"I know, but I believe it's better to get her into the habit now than to wait until she is older. How much do I owe you?" Anna asked, leading Penny into the kitchen.

Penny shook her head. "A cup of kaffe."

"Penny, you can't keep sewing for me for free," Anna insisted.

"I don't sew for free; I sew for kaffe. Besides, it gave me a gut excuse to come and visit you." Penny said, scooping up Joseph from where he was playing on a mat. "He's growing up too fast."

"I know, just yesterday he could barely smile. Now he's giving me trouble with his vegetables," Anna sighed fondly.

Penny sat down and let out a quiet sigh. She had spent most of the day packing and her back was aching from all the work. "And soon he'll be running around and you'll be protecting him from everything that might harm him."

"Exactly," Anna laughed. "You look tired, Seth, working you to the bone?"

Penny shook her head. "Not at all. He's actually been very kind. Insisting on helping me every day, while he's paying me to do the work."

"How long will you be working for him?" Anna asked curiously.

Penny shrugged. Today was her fourth day at Seth's father's house. "I'm not sure, but if I had to guess, I think I'll have everything packed by Friday, which only leaves the cleaning for next week."

"Is there so much to pack?"

Penny laughed. "That and more. It's as if the Mast family only moved everything they didn't use to the hayloft over the years. I've just about finished packing the cupboards in the house, except for the kitchen and the living room of course, but the hayloft... There are moth-eaten linens, old crockery and cutlery... it's as if everything just accumulated and accumulated over the years. I can understand why the task was a little intimidating for Seth to do alone."

"Sounds... interesting. And how are you.... With Seth?" Anna asked.

Penny thought for a moment and shrugged. "If you're asking if I have closure, then the answer is no. Seeing him again only reminds me of what we could've had. He never got married..."

Anna's eyes widened. "He isn't courting, either?"

Penny shook her head. "Nee, he hasn't courted in the last five years... Anna, what does that mean?"

"You're asking if it means if he still has feelings for you? Only you know that, Penny," Anna smiled kindly. "Do you still have feelings for him?"

"I don't think I'll ever forget Seth. If that means I still have feelings for him, then perhaps, jah. But he... he has said nothing, but we've had a moment. A moment where the time we lost disappeared. Where it was just the two of us again. Where everything seemed easy and it was like it used to be."

"You had a moment with him?" Anna asked, surprised. "Why are you only telling me this now? Does that mean you want to try again?"

"I don't know," Penny sighed. "I don't know if he's staying. I don't know if he feels the same. I don't even know if he wants to court me again. I just... I don't know. It's exhausting to be honest. Spending every day with him and trying to forget what we meant to each other..."

"And then, of course, there is Mary Yoder. She was all but throwing herself at him after Sunday service," Anna commented wryly.

"I know, I saw." Penny didn't expand on the way her eyes had met Seth's.

"Penny, can I give you a little advice?" Anna asked.

Penny nodded. If anyone can give me advice, it's you."

"Then listen carefully. You already gave Seth up once. If you really, really think he is the love of your life, don't let him slip away this time. Fight for what you have. Fight for what you could have. Don't let your father or anyone else stand in your way this time," Anna said with an urgency that made Penny pay attention.

"How do I fight for someone that I'm not even sure wants to fight for me?"

"You pay attention. If Seth is still interested, you'll pick it up soon enough. Just… be careful, Penny. I can't stand to see you heartbroken again." Anna stepped closer and hugged Penny's shoulder.

Penny nodded. "Before I fight for anything, I need to know how he feels, and I simply don't have the courage to ask him."

"Then give it time. Time will tell," Anna promised. "Just like time will tell if John will ever get around to finding me another chest of drawers for Rebecca's room. I used her chest of drawers for Joseph, but now we're running short on space. John promised he'd find someone to build a new one, but he's yet to do it." Anna shook her head. "I'm grateful for the wunderbaar mann I have, but I'm not grateful enough to wait for months every time I need something urgently."

Penny frowned. "Do you need a carpenter?"

"Jah, but the one in town isn't available at the moment. And John isn't really trying to find anyone else."

"Why don't you have John talk to Seth? Seth is a carpenter. I'm sure he can help you," Penny suggested.

"Do you think he'll help with everything he has going on?"

Penny nodded. "I think he wouldn't mind the work. I've found him fidgeting with his old carpentry tools in the barn twice now. I think he's tiring of packing and revisiting his past all day, every day. It might be a welcome project."

"We'll pay him, of course, but…. You know what, no more buts. I'll have John go see him tomorrow."

"Gut." Penny nodded as she stood up. "I've got to get home. Denke for the kaffe."

"My pleasure, denke for the prayer kapp. And Penny..." Anna waited until Penny met her gaze. "Jah?"

"Listen to your heart."

Penny nodded with a smile. "First, I'll need to find its voice."

Chapter 19
When the Clouds Part

Seth stepped into the barn and glanced up at the hayloft.

With the house mostly dealt with, Penny had been spending the last two days trying to sort through years of accrued items that his family had stored there.

A smile curved Seth's mouth. He enjoyed having Penny around.

He couldn't help but wonder what their life together would've been like if her father hadn't stopped them from getting married. Would they have spent their days like this, working side by side? Seth had long since forgiven Penny's father for keeping them apart, but he couldn't help but feel cheated in some ways.

Seeing Penny again had brought back all those old feelings. It only made him realize again why he had proposed to her the first time. When he had searched her eyes the other day, Seth had seen the same longing in her gaze as he had felt all these years.

But that didn't mean they could just pick up where they had left off all those years ago.

A sigh escaped him as he moved to the workshop area of his father's barn. His father had never been a carpenter like Seth was, but he had enjoyed making things himself. Seth allowed his hand to glide over the working table as his eyes caught sight of the tools.

Every tool had a story for Seth.

Like the saw, it was the first one he had ever used. Seth would always remember the scent of wood and dust as he had tried to build his first chair. Of course, the chair had been a disaster with skewed feet and a wobbly seat, but it had given him something he had never experienced before.

A sense of purpose.

To create something that would be functional and last long after its owners had forgotten about the man who had made it.

Underneath the seat of the chair, Seth had still carved his name and the year. Something he still did to this day. His clients never knew about the signature he put on his items, but if they looked closely, they would find it. Sometimes at the back of a server or underneath a table, once he had even carved it beneath the handle of a rocking chair.

This was his passion, what he used to clear his mind and to shut out the world.

When John Miller saw him regarding a chest of drawers, Seth's first instinct had been to decline the commission. He was here to deal with his father's affairs so that he could get back to his workshop and his life in Indiana.

But then he realized how much he had missed working with wood for the last few weeks. He had accepted the commission with one request: the Millers request nothing more than the number of drawers and the size of the chest of drawers.

He wanted a project that would give him creative freedom. A project that would allow him to spend some time away from everything related to his father's affairs. Hopefully something that would help him clear his mind.

Seth had picked up the wood in town the day before and now it lay before him like an empty canvas, waiting for him to turn it into something timeless. He already had a vision of what he wanted to create. All he needed to do now was to bring it to life.

He reached for a measuring tape and a pencil and, before he knew it; he was lost in the process.

"I'm glad you took on the job." Penny's voice interrupted him.

Seth looked up and his breath caught. With the light from the barn door shining behind her, it looked as if there was a halo around her. Until that moment, Seth hadn't been sure whether he should pursue Penny again, but with clarity like never before he realized he would regret it for the rest of his life if he didn't try.

"Jah, it's gut to be working again. Sitting around and sorting through things has become quite tedious."

Penny laughed. "Tedious but necessary."

"Jah," Seth nodded.

"I didn't think you'd take it on. You must be in a hurry to return?" Penny asked curiously.

Seth shrugged. "Not too much."

How did he tell her how he felt? How did he tell her he wanted to court her again? Seth found himself at a loss for words.

"Have you found a buyer for the house yet?"

Seth had been putting off returning the realtor's calls. He had left a message for Seth every day over the last couple of days. Seth wasn't sure if he was procrastinating because he wanted the house ready before showing it again or if he was having doubts about selling it. "Nee, not yet."

"Alright, well I'm off. I'll see you tomorrow. I ought to finish in the hayloft then."

Seth's eyes widened with surprise. "What time is it?"

"Just after four pm." A soft chuckle escaped her. "You've been at it all day. You didn't stop for lunch even."

Seth dragged a hand through his hair. "I forget about time when I work."

"I can see that. If there's nothing else you need me to do, I'll be done when the hayloft is finished."

The thought of Penny not coming around anymore made Seth's heart stop for a moment. "I'm sure there is more..."

"Seth, what still needs to be done? You can manage on your own. Although I'm grateful for the work, I don't want you to waste your money."

"It won't be a waste of money if it means I get to see you every day." The words escaped before he could stop them.

Penny's eyes widened slightly with surprise. Their gazes met and held. Seth wished he had the right words, the right way of saying them, to make Penny understand how he felt about her.

For a few moments they just stood there, neither sure what to do.

Penny finally smiled at him and said goodbye before she turned and walked out of the barn.

Seth saw his future flash before his eyes; images of him and Penny living on his father's property. Of them spending their days together and meals around the kitchen with laughing children.

His future wasn't in Indiana, his future was right here in Lancaster County.

His future was with Penny.

He just needed to make Penny see that. Seth rushed after her, but stopped at the barn door. The last time he had asked Penny to share her future with him, she had sent him away the following day.

This time he didn't want her to reconsider, or to have anyone change her mind. Before he approached her, he needed to be sure his affairs were in order and that he was willing to move back to Lancaster County.

Seth turned around and headed back to the chest of drawers. He glanced around the barn and wondered if he could turn it into the workshop he had in Indiana. It wouldn't be practical to ship all his things here, but perhaps if he sold them and bought new ones, it would work.

Instead of focusing on the chest of drawers, Seth wandered around the barn, considering his options. He couldn't come back to Lancaster County if there wasn't a demand for a carpenter.

If he couldn't be a carpenter, he wouldn't be able to care for his family.

Before he could even consider courting Penny again, Seth realized he needed to make sure he was able to do so.

He smiled, knowing that a lot of work and research lay ahead, but if it meant a future with Penny, he would do all the research needed before moving his life, his carpentry workshop, and his heart back to Lancaster County.

Chapter 20
Arguments of the Past

Penny had said goodbye yesterday.

He had no more work for her to do and she refused to waste his money by pretending to have work just to spend more time with him.

If working for Seth had been meant to give her closure, it had done the exact opposite. It had opened old wounds and brought back feelings she had tried her best to forget.

She had spent the night crying for the life they could've had and had and woken up with a headache, feeling even more confused than before. Just the thought of Seth leaving made her heart sink into the soles of her shoes.

If there had been nothing, not even a hint of his feelings for her, it would've been easier to say goodbye a second time. But deep-down Penny knew there was still something between them. When he looked at her in that way where the world disappeared, she could feel it.

But neither of them had spoken about it, nor the past.

Which meant in Penny's opinion, that was where Seth wanted to leave it.

With no sewing to do, Penny had spent the morning catching up with chores around the house. She had the afternoon free, but couldn't summon the energy or the willpower to spend it in the kitchen garden.

She needed to spend it alone.

She needed to make peace with Seth's return and his imminent departure for Indiana. Seeing him every day had been such a blessing, but now that the work was done it felt more like a curse.

She missed him.

More than she could ever express in words.

After clearing the lunch dishes, Penny took a walk down to the creek. The wind was cool, but she would endure it for a little peace.

As she walked to the creek, many memories came pouring back. She and Seth had visited the creek together too often to even remember. In summer they spent afternoons there with their feet in the water. In winter they would watch the melt trickle, trying its best not to be frozen solid. Penny had never thought of it as *their* place, but today she realized it was exactly that.

She hardly ever came to the creek on her own, especially not since the day of her baptism. But today the creek was what she needed to find a path through her muddled thoughts. To look towards her future and to stop yearning for the past.

Penny made her way through the thick brush that grew alongside the creek and smiled when she saw the water. The sun beams danced on the water in the late afternoon sun. Birds sung in a choir even as the leaves rustled to create a soft melody in the background.

Penny drew in a deep breath and felt calm wash over her as she took a seat beside an old fallen tree. It was too cold to dip her feet in the water, but that didn't mean she couldn't enjoy the freshness.

She leaned forward and touched the stream, careful not to topple over and fall in.

"Careful, you'll fall in."

Penny turned towards the sound of Seth's voice and lost her balance. Seth grabbed her arm just before she fell into the water. Once he was sure she was on steady footing, he let go of her arm.

"What are you doing here?" Penny asked, confused.

Seth shrugged. "Except for saving you?"

"You didn't save me," Penny snapped. She couldn't help but be agitated by his presence. How was she supposed to forget about him when he was everywhere? "I wouldn't have lost my balance if you didn't startle me."

Seth smiled. "Perhaps." He took a seat on the leaf bed and smiled up at Penny. "It's still as beautiful as I remember it. Beautiful and quiet."

Penny nodded and sat down a short distance from him. "That's why I'm here, for the quiet."

Seth nodded. "Do you remember how many afternoons we sat here by the old tree stump?"

"Jah." Penny didn't expand on her memories. They hurt enough without repeating them out loud.

"We were so young, weren't we?" Seth turned to her with a curious look.

"We were," Penny agreed.

"And yet I still dream of the same things we spoke about," Seth's voice had softened.

Penny frowned. Did he mean a family and a home, or did he mean a family and a home with her, like they had dreamed about? All this dancing around her feelings was exhausting, but she didn't dare reveal her feelings to Seth.

"Do you remember what we spoke about?" Seth asked.

Penny turned to him and shook her head. "That was a long time ago, Seth."

Seth laughed. "I know, the years simply flew by and you…only became prettier."

"Seth don't…" Penny warned him. She couldn't have him steal her heart, only to leave again.

"Don't what? Don't talk about the best time of my life? Don't compliment you?"

"Just… don't." Penny repeated with a heavy sigh.

"Why not, Penny? Because you still have those dreams?" Seth asked, searching her gaze.

Penny felt the tears well in her eyes and shook her head. "Nee."

Seth's mouth curved into a smile. "You always were a terrible liar."

Penny had been patient, had tried to be strong, but all of her resolve simply crumbled. "Why are you doing this? Why do you want to talk about back then? None of that matters anymore. Even if it still mattered, you're just going to leave again, just like you did last time."

"Penny, I left because it had all been arranged. I left to do my apprenticeship; I didn't leave you," Seth insisted. "Besides, you broke off our engagement."

"I broke it off because my daed told me to. You could've stayed, Seth, or at least have come back and fought for what we had. Instead, you ran away, all the way to Indiana, and I was here, brokenhearted and alone." Penny felt the tears coming close to spilling over her cheeks.

"You were here, alone? Penny, you should've stood up to your daed. You should've fought for us. You might have felt alone, but I was in Indiana without a single friend to talk to. And do you know what the worst part was? You *were* my best friend."

"Then I guess that doesn't apply anymore, so why bother talking to me then?" Penny demanded.

Seth let out a huff. "Because there are things I need to say."

"You know what? You just ruined the peace and quiet for me. I will not sit here and rehash the past. I have more important things to do." Penny stood up, brushed the leaves off her dress, and stomped through the brush.

Only once she arrived home, she realized she might have overreacted a little. But she refused to apologize. She had gone to the creek to clear her mind, not have Seth messing with it all over again.

And then to leave for Indiana.

Again.

Chapter 21 – Not For Sale

Seth stomped all the way home, furious and upset with himself.

He hadn't been prepared to see Penny at the creek. He had gone there to clear his mind and to try to find the right words to have Penny look at him again like she once did.

Instead, he found himself faced with the source of his problems, or his hope, and had fumbled through the stormy waters he had found himself in.

Why did he have to pry?

Why couldn't he just sit there quietly, and just be there with her?

He had just finished the chest of drawers for the Millers that morning and when he had delivered it, the joy on their faces had been exactly what he had hoped for. With his woodwork, he always won customers over, but with Penny….

It wasn't as easy.

Seth was about to make himself a cup of strong coffee when he heard an Englisch car pull up in the yard. He glanced out the window an recognized the realtor.

With a heavy sigh, he opened the door and waited for the realtor on the porch.

"Good afternoon Mr. Mast," Brandon Williams greeted him with a smile.

"Hullo, Mr. Williams," Seth nodded in greeting.

He showed Mr. Williams to the kitchen, where he offered him a cup of coffee.

Once Seth joined him at the table, Mr. Williams was all but brimming with excitement. "I have good news, Seth. Good news and great news. Which would you like to hear first?"

Seth cocked a brow, not eager to play games. "You decide."

"I have a buyer that would like you to accept their offer to purchase today, without even seeing the property. It's an elderly couple from Ohio, that wants to move to Lancaster County to be closer to their family. They're Amish, so that's a bonus," Williams rambled off.

Seth knew he was supposed to be overjoyed, but instead, he felt agitated.

"And!" Williams paused for effect. "They want to pay cash. No loans, nothing. So as soon as you accept their offer, I can get the ball rolling and get you back to Indiana."

Seth tilted his head, surprised by how uninterested he felt. This was the moment he had been waiting for. This was the offer he had hoped for and now that it was here, he couldn't for the life of him see himself selling his father's property.

He couldn't just sign away his childhood memories, he couldn't just leave Lancaster County.

Not again.

He shook his head and sighed. "I'm sorry if I wasted your time, Mr. Williams, but I would like to take the property off the market."

"What?" Brandon asked, surprised. "But the offer, it's perfect."

"I know, and I appreciate the effort you've gone through. I'd be happy to pay you for your time, but unfortunately, the property is no longer for sale."

Seth could see Brandon was ready to try to convince him otherwise, but Seth wasn't interested in contradicting arguments. He stood up and started towards the door, giving Brandon no choice but to follow.

"Are you sure you're doing the right thing? An offer like this doesn't cross your path every day."

Seth nodded. "This is what I want to do. Again, thank you for your time."

As soon as he closed the door behind the realtor, Seth felt an enormous weight lifted off his shoulders. He hadn't realized how much selling his father's property had bothered him until now.

He wasn't sure of what the future held, but for now he could only hope and pray it held all the dreams he had once shared with Penny.

He headed back inside and found a pen and a piece of paper before he began to write. He didn't even intend to give Penny the letter, he just needed to put his feelings and his hopes into words. Perhaps then if he saw her again he wouldn't have such a hard time expressing himself.

But as he wrote the letter, Seth felt hope swell in his chest. He would give Penny the letter and then he would wait.

Chapter 22
A Declaration of Honesty

After another night of tossing and turning as the past haunted her and the future taunted her, Penny felt ragged the next morning. She was quiet over breakfast, eager to get started with the day's chores. To busy her mind and her hands, she had washed all the windows today.

After sweeping the porch and doing all the regular chores, Penny went to check the mailbox like she did most mornings out of habit.

A white envelope without a postmark waited for her in the mailbox. She picked it up and curiously turned it over to see her name written on the front. Unsure what it was or who it was from, Penny opened it and took out the letter inside.

As she read she felt her knees weaken and hot tears stream over her cheeks.

My dearest Penny

I find myself writing this letter because in your presence, I struggle to find the right words to reveal how I feel about you.

I know that many years have passed since we became engaged. I know that talking about the past won't change anything, but I hope you have the patience to continue reading this letter.

That afternoon when I asked for your hand in marriage, we had our whole lives in front of us. We had spoken so often about what we wanted from our lives that I never once doubted we couldn't have it all. I saw my future entwined with yours.

You held my heart and my love, and I wouldn't have wanted it any other way.

When you broke off our engagement the following morning, it broke me.

Perhaps I should've argued, I should've forced you to go against your father, or perhaps I should've even encouraged you to run away with me to Indiana, but I didn't. I've regretted that every day since.

The reason I didn't do any of that is because I know how much you care for and respect your parents. I didn't want to be the reason for conflict in your familye. I didn't want you to choose between them or me. In a way, I understood why you chose them over me.

We were young then, but I believe we are wiser now.

When I saw you for the first time when I returned, it felt as if all the scars that remained from our breakup were scratched open with sharp claws. I was once again reminded of what we once had and I realized that I never found the right woman in Indiana, because none of them were you.

Penny, you were and always have been the only love of my life.

I've tried to convince myself otherwise so many times I've lost count. When I mistook John Miller for your husband and his kinner as yours, it felt as if someone had stolen my breath away never to return it again. It was the worst kind of pain I had ever imagined.

For a moment in time, I thought you were living the life you dreamed of with me with someone else.

I don't want to rehash the past like you said. I just want to be clear about how I felt back then.

I need to be even clearer about how I feel now.

I built a life for myself in Indiana, a gut life. But my life feels empty and as if it needs substance, because you aren't there to share it with me.

Having you around over the last couple of weeks only established again what I feared it would. My feelings for you never changed.

My feelings for you are stronger than they were when I asked for your hand in marriage all those years ago. When I look at you, Penny, I see my entire life unfold before me.

I see the dreams we dreamed by the creek realized and I feel as if there is purpose to all this time that has been lost.

When I courted you before, I had nothing to offer you but my heart. Penny, this time I can offer you home, a mann that will care for you, and I am wise enough to understand most of the challenges life has sent my way.

I ask you to meet me by the creek at three o'clock.

I want to court you again, Penny. Please don't hesitate. I won't be returning to Indiana, except to pack up my things and to move my workshop. I am staying in Lancaster County, in my daed's house. This is where I belong, with you.

Please Penny, my love for you never failed and never will. Meet me at the creek and give me a chance to prove to you how much you mean to me.

I've made mistakes and I've been hesitant to reveal my feelings to you, but I assure you I am ready to reveal them now.

I hope to see you there, at our spot.
Seth

Penny's heart soared with joy. If she had any doubt about how Seth felt about her, those doubts had been eased now. She glanced at the sun and wished it would make its journey through the sky a little quicker today, because she couldn't wait to see Seth at three o'clock.

Chapter 23
A Quick Proposal

Seth was too nervous to sit, instead he paced up and down the side of the creek while he waited to see if Penny would come. He was early and didn't expect her for at least another ten minutes, but that didn't stop him from keeping an eye out for her.

While he waited, his mind played mean tricks on him. What if she didn't check the mailbox? What if she didn't feel the same way about him anymore? What if she didn't want to spend the rest of her life with him?

By the time he heard footsteps crunch through the leaf bed, his hands were clammy with sweat, his heart racing a mile a minute with anticipation.

She stepped through the brush and Seth felt that familiar calm wash over him at the sight of her. A smile hesitantly curved his mouth as he moved towards her. "You came."

Penny nodded. "You asked."

"Did you get my letter?" Seth chuckled nervously. "You would've otherwise you wouldn't be here."

Penny smiled. "I got it. Thank you for writing it."

The air was thick with anticipation, the past and the present colliding at once.

"Penny I..." Seth began.

Penny held up her hand and stopped him with a shake of her head. "You had your turn. Now it's my turn. You're right, I didn't want to stand up to my parents. I was afraid if I did, they would blame me for the rest of my life. I haven't spent a day since not regretting it. But even if I stood up to them, Seth, you're right, I might have blamed you for being the wedge between us."

Seth nodded.

"Seeing you again, working for you… it brought back so many memories. It was harder than I thought it would be. I thought my feelings for you had faded away, but they hadn't. Instead, they are stronger than ever before. I simply tried to ignore them because I couldn't stand the thought of losing you again."

"Penny…"

Penny continued without giving Seth a chance. "My parents might have done what they thought was right, but now it's my turn. Seth, you're right for me and I want to give us another chance. I want to dream of our future by the creek. I want to commit my life to loving you and caring for you and I want to make up for all the time we lost."

Seth's heart skipped a beat with joy. "Really?"

Penny nodded. "I haven't been more certain of anything else in my life. I will never love another man the way I love you, Seth."

Seth felt a smile curve his mouth even as he kneeled down on one knee. He looked up at Penny and loved her more than ever before. "Penny Hershberger, I've courted you before but I never had the chance to be your mann. I don't want to waste more time by courting you. I know everything about you there is to know. I know your heart is kind, your soul is gentle and that you are hardworking. I know you will make me happy and that you will be a wunderbaar mamm. Penny, would you accept my hand in marriage?"

Penny's laughter flowed over Seth like a cleansing breath of air. "Jah, I will marry you, Seth. And this time..." a frown creased her brow, making her look cute as she tried to find the right words. "I'm not sure how it goes, but this time, let no man part what Gott has joined. Because I believe in my heart that Gott brought us back together."

Seth stood up and pulled Penny into his arms. He couldn't have said it better himself. She fit against him like a glove. Her slight frame made him feel strong and protective. Seth smiled into her neck, knowing he would never let her go again.

His eyes widened with fear as he pulled back and met her gaze. "What about your parents?"

Penny nodded heavily. "I know. Perhaps this time we should tell them together?"

Seth couldn't agree more. "Do you think now is a suitable time?"

Penny laughed. "No better time than the present."

Hand in hand, they walked back to Penny's home, picking up exactly where they had been broken off so long ago. If Seth had known that coming back to Lancaster County would give him a second chance with Penny, he would've returned a long time ago.

But now, in the fading light of the afternoon, he understood everything happened at the right time. Perhaps if he came back sooner, things might not have been the way they are now.

Gott's time, he reminded himself.

Everything happened in Gott's time.

Chapter 24
The Lion's Den

"There you are. I was just wondering where you were off to. Did you go visit with…?" Sarah Hershberger's words trailed off as she saw who followed her daughter into the kitchen.

"Hullo Mamm. Is Daed around?" Penny asked, squaring her shoulders.

At the surprised look on her mother's face, she couldn't help but fear that this would be a repeat of their conversation when Seth had asked for her hand the first time.

"I uh… I think he's in the barn."

Penny nodded. "Mamm, would you please fetch him? Seth and I have something we would like to talk to you about."

Penny would've offered to fetch her father herself, but after the way her parents had driven them apart the last time, she refused to be separated from Seth until her parents had heard them out.

Her mother frowned but set down the dish cloth she had been using. "Of course."

Once they were alone in the kitchen, Penny turned to Seth. "Kaffe?"

Seth laughed. "I hardly think this is going to be a social visit."

"Then we make it one," Penny insisted as she put on a fresh pot of coffee.

A few moments later, her parents returned, side by side. Penny couldn't help but feel slightly intimidated by their unity.

"Penny? What is going on?" her father asked, glancing first at Penny and then at Seth.

Penny drew in a deep breath. She looked at Seth for courage before she returned her gaze to her father's. "Seth and I are getting married as soon as the bishop will let us."

Her mother's jaw dropped, but her father's expression didn't change.

Before they could object, Penny began to talk. "I don't blame you for forcing me to break off our engagement before. We were very young. But this time, we're not young. We know exactly what we are doing. We love each other, regardless of the time that has passed. I love both of you dearly, you know that, but I won't let you stand in our way again. If you want to disown me for following my heart, then that is your choice. But hope wholeheartedly that you will embrace my decision and offer us your blessing."

"Mr. and Mrs. Hershberger. I know this might come as a shock to you. Believe me, it came as a shock to both Penny and I that our feelings for each other hadn't changed. But I want to assure you I love your dochder. I can care for her, and I intend to remain in Lancaster County. Penny and I will live in my daed's home, close enough that you can spend time with your grandchildren. I'll protect her, provide and care for her until my dying breath. If that isn't enough to convince you how strongly I feel about your dochder, then I'm afraid nothing ever will be."

Penny nodded, appreciating Seth's input.

Her mother was clearly waiting for her father to say the first word. She remained frozen in the spot. Not even her expression changed.

Penny feared her father would turn them both away, but instead of saying anything, he sat down at the kitchen table. He glanced at her mother before he turned back to Seth. "Have a seat. I smell fresh kaffe brewing."

Penny and Seth shared a confused look. Seth did as he was told, while Penny served everyone a cup of coffee. When she joined her parents and Seth at the table, her father let out a heavy sigh.

"I owe both of you an apology." Her father's voice was heavy. "Before… I still saw Penny as my little girl. I knew you loved each other, but I was afraid you were too young. It took me about a year to realize that I might have ruined Penny's future with my decision."

Her father turned to her and reached for her hand. "Penny, I've watched you all these years, content but not happy. It broke my heart to know that I had caused that. If I was a more courageous man, I might have gone to see Seth in Indiana, but I was afraid meddling more might make things even worse… for both of you."

Penny shook her head, confused. "What do you mean?"

"I mean Seth is right. You've lost enough time. He's a gut mann, one that will provide for you and care for you. I give you my blessing to be married. I'll even ask the bishop to make it soon myself."

Penny's laughter filled the air even as Seth let out a sigh of relief.

"I'm so happy for you, dochder. You deserve all this happiness and more," her mother said, reaching for her other hand.

Penny felt tears of joy well in her eyes. She had been prepared to fight for their love, instead her father had admitted to his mistake. It wasn't a triumph to hear her father apologize, but it was an ointment to the wounds she had been nursing all these years. She turned to Seth and smiled brightly. "I guess we're getting married."

"Jah," Seth agreed happily. "And once we're married, we can travel to Indiana together to pack up my life there. I'm never letting you go again, not even for a couple of days."

Penny laughed. "I'm sure I'll be fine for a few days on my own."

"He's right. You have so much time to make up for. Go with him. You can spend your honeymoon creating your life together, and perhaps even doing some sightseeing along the way," Sarah encouraged.

Seth nodded and turned to her father. "Mr. Hershberger, I know you are a proud man, but I also know that things have been tight with the last harvest. I would like you to consider me investing in your farm. Not a large sum, just enough to tide you over until the next harvest. That way, Penny and I have some interest in your farm and you can rest assured that I will always be there to support you or help you when you need it."

Penny held her breath. Seth had mentioned nothing about offering her father money. She couldn't help but fear that Seth's good intentions might just ruin their brief triumph.

Her father thought for a long moment before he held out his hand to Seth. "Welcome to the familye. I'll gladly accept your investment, after all, this farm isn't just Penny's future, it is now yours as well."

Penny couldn't help but be baffled and surprised as Seth and her father shook hands.

Her second chance had finally arrived and Penny just knew that this time it was going to be perfect.

Epilogue

"I don't know how you do it," Penny said with a sigh as she joined Anna on the porch.

Anna laughed and held up her cup of tea. "Lots of tea, patience, and prayer."

"Anna, it's only ten o'clock in the morning and I'm already exhausted. I'm so busy between the chores and taking care of Matthew and cooking that I get nauseous because I don't even get time to eat," Penny admitted with a shake of the head.

Anna's son Joseph had just turned five a few weeks ago and simply adored playing with Penny and Seth's son, Matthew, who was now two years old. Ever since he had walked, he seemed to only know one speed – running.

"You've had a busy few years. Maybe it's time to slow down and smell the roses a bit," Anna suggested.

Penny shook her head. "I haven't had time to prune the roses, so I doubt there will be any this year."

Anna laughed. "Penny, in a matter of three years, you moved into this house, made it your own, became pregnant, had a son who suffered from colic until he was twelve months old, and you've been doing chores and sewing between all the sleepless nights and rushing from one chore to the next. If having four children has taught me anything, it's resting when they're quiet and to sleep when they sleep, even if that is a midmorning nap."

"A mid-morning nap sounds wunderbaar right about now," Penny yawned.

Anna was right. It had been a very busy three years for her. But she wouldn't exchange it for a moment's peace. Getting married to Seth and spending two months travelling as they made their way back to Lancaster County had been chaotic but memorable.

Moving into his father's home and making it their own had been hard work for both of them. Seth had to install his workshop into the barn. His father's workshop simply wasn't adequate for all the intricate furniture commissions Seth received.

Then there was the kitchen garden, helping her parents on their farm, and of course there was Matthew.

"Penny, perhaps you should see the doctor. Is something wrong?" Anna asked curiously.

Penny shook her head. "Nee, I'm sure I'm just busy."

Anna laughed and shake her head. "Or you're with child again. Have you considered that?"

Penny's eyes widened. She quickly did the math in her mind and realized she'd been so focused on Matthew and everything else she hadn't even realized she was two months late. "Nee, it can't be, can it?"

Anna smiled warmly and reached for Penny's hand. "It definitely can be. Why don't you call for an Englisch driver and go buy one of those home pregnancy tests the Englisch use, at least then you'll know. I'll look after the boys while you're gone."

"Don't you have to get back to the twins and Rebecca?"

"They're in school for another three hours. Go on," Anna encouraged her.

A few hours later, Penny stood in the kitchen waiting for Seth to come in for lunch. He usually skipped lunch when he was busy, but Penny simply couldn't wait until that evening to tell him. When an hour passed, she put down Matthew for his nap before she went in search of her husband.

She found him in the workshop, carving something into the seat of a rocking chair. "What's that?"

Seth smiled as if she had caught him. "It's a secret."

Penny narrowed her gaze with a teasing smile. "I have a secret, too. Tell me yours and I'll tell you mine."

Seth gestured her to come closer and showed her. Penny looked at Seth's name carved into the wood alongside the year. "What is that?"

"It's something I put on all my pieces. I don't tell the clients about it, and it's usually hidden, like with this rocking chair it will be beneath the seat, where no one will see it."

"How clever. That way you get to live on through your furniture forever."

Seth nodded. "I knew you'd understand. Now, your turn."

Penny shrugged. "My secret is almost like yours. It's hidden. No one can see it, but it will live on long after I'm gone."

Seth frowned, "Are you talking about the dust beneath the woodstove? I told you I can't move it on my own."

Penny laughed. "Not the dust, Seth, I don't care if it stays there forever. In fact, it's our dust, we'll make sure to take care of it."

"Then what is it?" Seth asked, confused.

Penny reached for his hand and laid it on her belly. "Another blessing from Gott."

Seth's eyes widened with surprise and joy. "We're having another boppli?"

Penny nodded. "Jah, I'm about two months along. I'll have to go see the Englisch doctor to be sure, but that's why I've been so tired all the time."

Seth scooped her up and twirled her in a circle before he set her down. "Do you know what, Penny? I always imagined our future together would be wunderbaar, but the truth is, it's even better than I ever could've imagined."

Penny nodded and hugged her husband. "I think it's about to get even better."

*** The End ***

Thank you kindly for choosing to read my book. I sincerely hope you enjoyed it. All of my Amish Romances are wholesome stories suitable for all to enjoy.

If you could be so kind to leave a review on Amazon, I would appreciate it.